# That Woman's Husband
## A Skye Novel

Keima Campbell

ISBN: 0615764924
ISBN-13: 978-0615764924

# DEDICATION

This book is dedicated to my four children Aminah Cottle, Ariyah Cottle, McCoy Jones, and Miriam Finch, my best friend Tyauna Anthony may you R.I.P you taught me what being a TRU friend and sister meant, and to my little brother DeAngelo Lytton aka Booder R.I.P. baby boy not a day goes by that I don't miss you.

# ACKNOWLEDGMENTS

First and foremost I want to acknowledge God and thank Him for providing me with such a wonderful gift, the strength and courage to follow my dreams, and for allowing me the ability to share my talent with others. To my mother Sheryl Campbell thank you for always believing in me even when I didn't believe in myself and encouraging me during this long journey called life. I love you mom. I also want to say thanks to my grandparents Russell and Sally Jones for being the best grandparents ever. I look at you two as my second parents and love you dearly. To my Aunt Yolanda Carr and Uncle Milton Carr for as long as I can remember I could always count on you too to help guide me and give me good advice when I didn't want to go to anyone else with my problems. I love you two and encourage you to keep moving forward despite any trials and tribulations you experience. To my little brothers Vonnie, Kevin, and Debo, and my little sister TT Mama ya'll know you have always been my babies even though you are grown. I taught you all a lot and you taught me a lot too. I am the oldest I appreciate you allowing me to boss you around from time to time even in your old age. Love you guys. To all my supporters, family and friends Kandra Poole, Latrice Parks-Gold (whatever you call yourself these days. You know I had to mess with you), Imani Smith, Fitema Hamilton, Kim Hall, Kim Brown, Shannoil Clark, Cynthia Sannon, Tunieka Hicks, Jimmy Sidor just to name a few I love you guys and appreciate you giving it to me raw during this whole process. Thanks to my Uncle Daniel Campbell and his wonderful wife Allie Campbell thank you for loving me and supporting me. Uncle thanks for helping me drive to Atlanta even though you were a Cub Scout lol. Anyone I missed I am so sorry but know I love and appreciate your help and support as well. To Kenny Smith thank you for always asking have you been writing today? No? Why not? How much did you get done? Where are you at with this? I appreciate you being as excited about this as me. Thank you! To a very special guy Corey Smith aka Solomon I have to acknowledge you because without you I would have never made it this far. You helped me out of something that I thought was bigger than me and showed me what living was really about and I love you dearly for that..

# AVA

## (1)

I'd just gotten home from a long day at work. I didn't know what it was about me or how things had gotten so out of control but Dr. Harold Mitchell and I were not seeing eye to eye. I did my job, matter of fact I did my job better than just about anyone in the ER but his ass was constantly barking orders at me. Always finding something that he felt I could and should do better. Sighing looking at the clock I couldn't believe how things had went down. It was enough that I had to go through bullshit with Rodney my children's father every damn day of the week I'd be damned if I let my work invade my thoughts while I lay across my bed inside my cozy room and in my own damn house.

I didn't feel like cooking so I'd stopped and picked up a couple pizzas on my way home from a very short day at work. My nerves were getting the best of me so I sipped on a glass of wine just to relax for the evening. If I was a weak woman I would have snapped a long time ago taking out all the ignorant men in my life and not thought twice about it until I was locked up in a prison cell left with only me, my thoughts, regrets and a big bitch named Bertha trying to get my nookie.

People sure knew how to push me to my limit. I glanced at the clock again 6:30 p.m. just five minutes past the last time I took a peek. Rodney should have had the kids' home two hours ago. But of course who I was I fooling I couldn't depend on him for anything. Never could with the exception of a good fight for my life.

At some point I must have fallen asleep because I found myself being awakened by Jaquan running through the house screaming for his mommy. I sat up thinking finally they are home almost four hours later but at least I didn't get the call that I'd have to come pick them up because their father and his girlfriend had gotten into a fight and she took her car. Shaking my head I walked into the hallway running into a big hug from my son. He was by far the greatest little guy in the world. He was my heart my little king and I loved him dearly. I picked him up hugging him tightly and snuggling my nose into his neck causing him to giggle and try to slide out of my arms.

I put him down and made my way down the hallway descending the stairs where I found my daughters and their father. Letting out a deep sigh I approached trying to stay as cordial as possible. Rodney and I had been together for a very long time. We had a toxic relationship I don't know how many black eyes and busted lips he'd given me way more than I could even think to count. I wasn't sure how many times he'd cheated on me either and tried to convince me that I was the one sleeping around. He was the worst kind of man a woman could ever be involved with. Insecure and cowardly. He didn't love himself never had. I'd tried to play the heart mender only to be run down into the murky waters of the swamp of misery right along with him.

The saying, "hurt people hurt people" is one of the truest statements I've ever heard. Because his hurt was always made into mine physically, mentally, emotionally, spiritually, and financially I took an ass whipping whenever he felt like dishing me out one. While I was trying to love him I'd lost sight of myself and stopped loving me. Then again maybe I never really loved myself because if I did why would I stay in that relationship enduring nonstop abuse for so long? These were questions four years later I couldn't answer. Or why the hell did I continue to allow him back into my life time and time again just because he'd decide he was tired of being with whomever he was with and ready to come back home? Those times were over.

After the last time I let him back in and he went upside my head I made a vow I wouldn't take it anymore. What type of example was I setting for my daughters? Who would they look up to? What type of sorry ass boys in men's bodies would they call their husbands, boyfriends, and fiancés if I allowed them to continue to see such ignorance? Hell what type of husband would my son become? If I didn't leave for anything else that last ass whipping assured me it was time to leave for my kids.

I'll never forget him sitting over me, as my life flashed before my eyes and my son at seven years old running to my rescue knocking him out of a blind rage before he killed me. Sure I fought back but I was no match for a three time Golden Gloves Boxing Champion. He'd have a scratch here and there may be a bruise or knot but I always ended up being beaten badly piling on makeup trying to hide what everyone knew was going on. Life was too short and I refused to continue to live in misery and feed his self pity. We were done.

The look on Rodney's face caused me to twist my own into a contorted grimace. I knew the look I'd seen it far too many times and it made me sick to my stomach just thinking about what a fool I'd been for this monster of a man. He was going to ask me to come back home. Only this wasn't his home it was mine. He'd never paid one bill up in this bitch just leeched off of me for as long as he could. Never bought any food, deodorant, or soap up in this mothafucka. He didn't contribute one damn thing to this household.

"How are you doing?" I asked without making eye contact and attitude evident in my tone.

"Damn!" he started. "Is that how you greet your baby daddy?"

Just the sound of his ignorance made me want to punch him in his face. That baby daddy, baby mama shit was so ignorant and he knew it pissed me off but of course that was what he was there for, to make my life a living hell. I know because he did so every chance he got.

I looked up at him his eyes were low, red, and glossy. I could smell the liquor and weed reeking from his clothing and pores. He'd driven my children home drunk as a skunk and I mean fucked up! Needless to say I was angry as hell. Not only did he constantly put himself in harm's way but he'd taken it upon himself to drive my children our children home while under the influence of alcohol, marijuana and considering who I was dealing with who knew what else.

I could feel my blood began to boil and wanted to bang on his ass instead I took the grown woman approach as I politely asked Dominique and Antoinette to take their bags upstairs to unpack so they could get ready for school the next morning. I'd speak my words very carefully and use a little reverse psychology to get him out of my home without a fight.

As the girls retreated to their bedroom I put my plan into action. "Well," I began. "Thanks for bringing them home I really appreciate it but we have to start getting ready to settle down for the night. I have to help the kids get ready for school in the morning."

This fool had the nerve to ignore what I was saying and plop his stank ass down on my sofa and put his dirty ass shoes up on my coffee table. I took a deep breath and calmly asked him to remove his feet from my table. He continued to ignore me. I knew this shit was coming when I saw him standing in my house high as a kite. I'd made it a point to never let him come in because in his warped mind he always felt that was invitation to make himself comfortable in my home.

"Rodney!" I barked with a little more base in my voice. He cocked his head to the side looking at me with that cynical smirk on his face. "You need to get up and leave right now," I said lowering my tone but still remaining firm in what I was saying.

That's when all hell broke loose. He jumped up screaming and hollering how I thought I was better than him and how he wasn't going anywhere that this was his damn house and his kids. Out of nowhere he started asking if I was insinuating that they weren't his kids and that he knew I was a hoe when he started fucking with me. He should have left me right where I was shaking my ass for money. But the thing was I never needed him or his money I made more money shaking my ass than he did all week petty hustling. Once he realized that he stopped hustling altogether. I worked fulltime was a fulltime mother and went to nursing school fulltime.

That was his way of trying to bring me down but I wasn't ashamed of shit I did anymore. It made me the woman I am today. I am a damn good woman and mother if I might say so myself. I let him go into his little rage as I stood there smirking eyeing the brass candlestick holder sitting on my table. I didn't love his ass anymore I would bash his fucking face in if I made it to that candlestick before I got hurt too bad. Why should I even entertain these thoughts I questioned myself this man is out of his mind coming into my home and attempting to belittle me especially in front of my children who were now gathered together in a small huddle at the top of the stairs.

It seemed as if the calmness that surrounded me was making him angrier and that is when he became physical.

"Bitch don't you ever disrespect me in front of my kids!" he bellowed as he brought down his hand across the right side of my face. The sting of the blow was excruciating, it felt like flames, I could feel my face burning from the inside out or maybe it was the outside in. I could hear my children screaming Mommy and that is when the lioness in me came out and the fight was on. I kicked him in his nuts thinking it would buy me some time like it did on the movies but this monster had super strength he walked right through that shit. I tried to make a beeline for the candlestick holder but he snatched me by my long ponytail as I stretched out my arms trying to get away.

I could hear him laughing that evil ass laugh of his as I tried to get away, my children screaming, me yelling for them to call the police. I was sick of being quiet about this I was sick of him beating me whenever he pleased. We weren't together. One way or another I was done being nice because nice didn't get me anywhere with this asshole. I spotted his keys resting on the arm of the sofa snatched them up and rolled under his arm twisting my neck into an unnatural angle and clocked him in the side of his head.

He let out a scream releasing my hair. I didn't stop though I ran to the coffee table picked up the candlestick holder and just as he regained his composure and began to come after me I sent the brass decor crashing down on top of his head opening up a deep gash forcing him to let out an agonizing howl. I've never heard someone holler like that before and had it been anyone else I would have felt sympathy but it was Rodney my tormentor. I was outside of myself watching as I held my hand high bringing down my weapon again this time with the force of the universe behind me. There was hatred inside me I'd never allowed "ME" to become unleashed. I was ready to kill him.

My hand was stopped in midair. Within those few seconds I hadn't heard my children's screams or the policemen that had entered my home. My ear was still ringing from the punch he had delivered to my temple I was deaf!!!! Or temporarily deaf!!!! I didn't know but if this mothafucka made me handicapped I was killing him and anybody including the authorities who stood in my way.

I was struggling with the officer but he wasn't struggling with me. He'd actually manhandled me to say the least. He had my black ass on the ground face first with his knee in my back handcuffing me while his partner called for an ambulance. That was the first time Rodney ever needed an ambulance for himself. Even if I did go to jail for trying to kill his ass I'd still hold my head up high because this was really the beginning of a new beginning for me. I wasn't taking anyone's shit anymore, especially when they were putting my children's safety in jeopardy. It was enough he put his hands on me but the more I thought about everything I'd been through with him he'd terrorized my children just as much as he did me.

I could hear my children's voices in the background although I couldn't quite make out what they were saying. I am assuming they were explaining the situation to the asshole that had his knee dug deep into my back because before I knew it I was being snatched up and placed on the couch. I stared at the officer void of all emotion my chest heaving up and down. Now that I think back sista girl most definitely had lost all touch with reality at that moment. He spoke as I gave him a blank stare watching his lips move and not comprehending a word he was saying until my son ran up to me crying and placing his small arms around my neck.

My fucked up day had turned out far worse than it had started I wasn't sure if I was going to go to jail or not. Domestic violence was tricky these days. A woman could get her ass kicked for breakfast, lunch, and dinner for fifteen years trusting that her man was going to make a change and love her one day as much as she loved him but the instant she stood up for herself she was being hauled off to jail and sitting in some courtroom trying to make a jury of her peers understand that she'd endured far worse in her time in the relationship and it was literally a matter of life or death. Sure she didn't call the cops any time before then but how many battered women actually did?

"Ma'm?" The officer repeated with a concerned look on his face. I could hear the ambulance sirens blaring outside of my door and for the first time I noticed all that was left of Rodney was the bloodstain in my carpet. They had hauled him right on up out of there without me noticing.

Blinking a few times I was finally able to respond in a slow shaky whisper, "I would like to press charges," I said as tears streamed down my face. I was tired of fighting, tired of crying, tired of dealing with the father of my children and his violent outbursts. The officer went on to explain to me the process for situations like mine. He gave me some resources and told me how lucky I was that things hadn't ended worse. I wondered if he was speaking in terms of me killing him or him killing me. As horrible as this may sound I wished I had killed him. Officer Jackson told me Rodney was going to jail and handed me his card in case I had any other questions. Once he was gone I held the card tightly inside my hand as if my entire existence depended on it.

As the multitude of professionals who protected and served the citizens of my city slowly dispersed from my home I slowly came back to my senses. Everything had happened so fast I didn't have time to really consider what I was doing or trying to figure out an alternative way to handle the situation. I closed my front door watching as my neighbors walked back into their homes or began shutting their blinds because all the action was over.

*Nosey mothafuckas always in somebody else's business.* That's what my mind said. I wasn't mad at them though. I was angrier with myself for putting up with the nonsense and giving anyone a chance to gossip about me. Hell I wasn't even sure if they did talk about me. If so they probably talked about how much of a fool I was and how many times the police were at my home in the past six years. I'd lost count personally. I held my head down and retreated back to my living room.

I silently prayed thanking God that I was off work the following day or better yet prayed I still had a job when it was time to go back. Walking out and telling the boss you were taking a personal day because he had pissed you off wasn't exactly something that would keep you employed with an organization especially working in an emergency room that is already short staffed. Rolling my eyes I plopped down on my sofa knowing I had to get an order of protection immediately. I had never hurt Rodney in the past and truthfully I wasn't sure if he would come after me or not but better safe than sorry. Not saying that a small piece of paper would actually keep him away from me but I knew he didn't like jail and maybe he'd sit in there and have some time to really think about his actions. Maybe they'd order him to get some psychological help because he had serious problems with the functioning of his brain.

I sat there with my children gathered around their tear stained faces looking at me asking me mommy what is next? Their eyes pleading for that chapter in our lives to be over. I never wanted to be the woman to keep a man from his children but I had no choice. The hurt in their eyes caused by me staying in that situation for so long hurt me to the very pit of my stomach all I could do was shake my head from side to side as a fresh pool of tears cascaded down my face. How shameful of me to have subjected them to so much trauma. Not only was I shaking away the shame I was shaking away the memories and any feelings I once had towards the man I'd lain with for many years. That chapter in my life was officially over.

# AVA

## (2)

I'd gotten up early to start off my day. Although my children and I stayed up all night discussing the future of our family I had plenty things that needed to be done to get the process moving in order to get Rodney out of our lives. Surprisingly none of my children were opposed to the idea. Dominique my eldest daughter despised him, Antoinette feared him, and Jaquan just plain hated him. If my son had been old enough to protect me I knew he would have harmed his father a long time ago. As their mother it was my duty to show them love and peace.

I walked into the emergency department with my sunglasses hiding my swollen eyes. They had begun to turn pinkish/purple over night. I had tried to keep the swelling down as best as I could by applying ice. The pain I felt in my face was enough for me to opt out of putting on makeup to cover them up. The shades would have to do. Every time I thought about the events that had taken place I became angry. Who the hell did he think he was putting his hands on me?

Donna the triage nurse spoke to me as I strolled past the corner room searching for Dr. Mitchell. We had to have a talk. Although I had left work the previous day for totally different reasons I could remove my sunglasses for dramatic effect and plead my case. Truth was I'd been ashamed about my situation for a long time but now I had to keep my job and in doing so come clean. Losing my job was not an option.

As I approached Dr. Mitchell I began to get nervous. I hated when I acted on pure emotion. I was too old to be getting fired from a job especially one that had turned into a full blown career. I could feel the tension the closer I got to him. Small beads of sweat began to form underneath my nose. Pulling in a deep breath of air that smelled of sterilization and antibiotics I stood directly in front of Perry as he looked over a patients chart. I sure as hell didn't want all those women in my business and knowing that they weren't busy it wouldn't take much to get him into a private area to discuss what needed to be discussed which was my future at the hospital.

Without even looking up from the paperwork he called out to me, "How may I help you today Ms. Tanner?" his voice was so irritating. I didn't know if it was because I couldn't stand the man or if he really did shrill like a bitch every time he opened his mouth. Either way he most definitely made my skin crawl. I stood there for a moment taking in his entire being. He wouldn't be so bad looking if he didn't have such a funky attitude. He only stood about 5'10" tall, with beautiful brown skin, and a perfect set of white teeth. His hair was cut low in a temple fade he didn't sport any facial hair. You could tell that he worked out and the way he dipped when he walked told some stories of what he was possibly packing in the middle section. As soon as he opened his mouth all those good looks disappeared and he became the person I despised.

Apparently I didn't respond to his question fast enough because he started in on me in front of my co-workers and even a couple patients' family members who had recently been discharged and were leaving their rooms.

"Did you come into my ER this morning to throw another one of your little temper tantrums on your day off?" he spat at me. "I have a right mind to fire your ass on the spot right now but because we are short staffed and could use your help although your work lately has been less than competent it will be waiting for you when you come back I know you NEED your job to take care of all those children of yours." He added.

I could feel my blood start to boil as my lips pursed up and what I intended to do when I walked into that hospital almost went by the wayside and the police were going to be on my ass again because I had floored his ass. My co-workers continued doing what they were doing as if they hadn't heard a word. I knew they heard that bastard talking to me sideways but either out of fear or sheer ignorance they pretended as if they had not. Dr. Mitchell had a way of scaring people but not me I always gave him a run for his money. That's probably why he was always on my ass.

Closing my eyes briefly and counting to ten in my mind I began to speak, "Perry?" I knew that would make him mad. He always wanted to be referred to as doctor as if anyone calling him Dr. Mitchell gave him a secret kryptonite power that no one else possessed. Ssshhhhh negroe please you pull your pants down to shit just like everyone else. He was really crossing the line speaking of my children but I'd keep my cool….. For now. I'd come to apologize and that was exactly what I was going to do I didn't need any more problems.

Dr. Mitchell finally looked up from the chart he held in his hands. He was angry and it was that silent victory that kept my hands by my sides. There is more than one way to skin a cat and I was just that woman to become familiar with them all.

"Dr. Mitchell," he corrected me trying to put some bass in his voice. What a joke. He still sounded like a bitch.

"Oh excuse me, I mean Dr. Mitchell," I taunted. "Can I have a brief moment with you to discuss something in private?" I asked sarcastically.

With a simple grunt he started walking towards the small office space that was kept down the hall. I was sure he had a mouth full of things to say to me in private. I was also sure he would raise his voice loud enough for everyone to hear but I wasn't about to give him the time to get the upper hand or the satisfaction. I was getting the last word and there were no ifs ands or buts about it.

As soon as I closed the door behind me he started to speak the nonsense he always did. He is my superior and I will show him respect. Blah! Blah! Blah! He didn't give a damn how good of a nurse I was he would let me go. I slowly removed my glasses for dramatic effect showing him my swollen eyes and whipped up some of the tears I had cried the night before. I wasn't still upset I honestly felt all cried out about the situation but playing on his intelligence was something I enjoyed doing. Hopefully he had a heart and I'd bring him down a couple notches even if it was somewhat of a lie.

"Listen, Perry," I said looking at the doctor between swollen eyes. "This has been what I have been dealing with for many years," I said as I pointed to my wounded face as tears welled up in my eyes. To my surprise there was really emotion behind the crying after I started to speak. My voice was cracking and I could feel pressure mounting in my sinuses. "All I want to do is come here to do my job without you constantly harassing me," I continued. "I am thankful for this place I am grateful for the great people I work with. But would it hurt you to treat us like human beings?" I asked really putting out all I had to say without yelling, hollering or becoming angry.

Perry stared for a moment before he approached me and traced his hand over my red swollen eyes. For a moment his eyes softened as he took in the sight that was before him. He examined my entire body with his eyes noticing the scratches, scrapes, and bruises that had surfaced as a result of my altercation with Rodney.

He grabbed my hands and expressed how sorry he was and asked if there was anything he could do. I assured him I would be fine and thanked him for taking the time out to listen to me. At that point I had become so emotional that I began to cry on his shoulder. He took me in and before I had a chance to even realize what was taking place I could feel his strong hands rubbing my back as he held me. *Did I just hear a moan?* I tried to pull myself away slightly and but he pressed me into him tighter. Not enough to cause me to become alarmed but to let me know he didn't want me going anywhere.

I was completely taken aback when the assuring rubs became caresses. Was I getting sexually harassed? Or was I just so full of emotion I couldn't decipher the difference between someone attempting to help me and someone taking advantage of me? I asked myself these questions until I heard a second moan as Perry's hands moved down my back and began to caress my behind. His breathing was becoming erratic as he palmed my backside placing small kisses on my neck. For a moment I was frozen in time. I couldn't believe this was happening to me.

The past 24 hours had been crazy. I tried to push away this time with a little more force but he pulled me closer telling me to just relax I needed to feel loved. Here I was in this room at my place of employment work with one of the doctors I supported expressing to him the trauma I was enduring in my personal life and he was taking advantage of me, invading my personal space, fondling me. I didn't ask for that kind of treatment.

I pushed him away this time harder causing him to snap out of his lustful trance. "What in the hell is wrong with you Dr. Mitchell?" I exclaimed. This time I did not use his first name. He was right we were not on a first name basis and he'd obviously gotten things confused. He looked at me with a smirk on his face.

"What do you mean what's wrong with me, Ava?" he said adjusting the stiffness that had formed in his pants. "I know what you want even when you don't," he added with a slight chuckle.

Clearly disgusted I threw my hands in the air snatched the door open and stormed out of the office leaving my glasses sitting on the table. I could hear someone calling my name in the background I didn't stop. My legs wouldn't allow me to turn around they were wobbly like spaghetti noodles. I continued to press forward out of the double doors that led to the parking lot. I couldn't believe that son of a bitch had just sexually harassed me. I wanted to go to Human Resources and tell but then he could say I'd walked out yesterday and there went my job.

I'd played my card all wrong walked up in there on my day off, called the man by his first name in front of my co-workers, and lured him into the office with the door locked and closed. How would that look on my part? It would be his word against mine and I was tired of fighting I didn't have time for it. I would definitely be looking to secure another job in another facility this was way too much.

As I reached my car I felt a heavy hand press down on my shoulder. I spun around with my hands up ready to knock fire from Dr. Mitchell. I exhaled putting my guard down a little bit when I noticed it was Dr. Cameron Powers one of the sweetest people on earth. Just his presence alone was soothing.

He had a good aura about himself and was always nice and friendly.

"Hey Ava, "he said out of breath from chasing me down. He was such a handsome guy but married. Whoever she was she was a lucky woman. I'd have taken him over Rodney any day. Where did these women find these men at anyway? I always ended up with the thugs, playas, hustlas, hell I'd even dated a pimp in my lifetime. In between Rodney and me breaking up I'd get lonely and in came another loser.

"How are you doing Cameron?" I asked a little curter than I intended. Hell I was having a horrible day scratch that a horrible week.

"You're running up out of here Ms. Lady I know it's your day off and all but could you have at least stopped by and told a brotha hello?" he responded smiling showing all of his pretty teeth.

Let me say one thing about Cameron he was fine. He had the most beautiful skin it was naturally tanned and healthy looking. He was in his mid thirties but honestly didn't look a day over 22. He is what I like to call a pretty boy about 5'11" with a small build all muscle of course. His facial features were perfect with a little curl to his hair. The brotha always smelled good, looked good, and was pleasant. His presence was always welcomed from me except for today I wasn't in a very talkative mood.

I was trying to avoid eye contact on purpose. Damn! I had forgot my glasses and although I suspected that most of the people I worked with had saw me with a black eye or two and heard the lies I told about how I'd gotten them it was still embarrassing sporting the sins committed against me by Rodney on my face in front of everybody. I hated it, I hated that he had control over me even when he wasn't around.

"I'm sorry, Dr. Powers," I responded bringing myself back to reality. I'd just set myself up for nonsense I'd be damned if I did it again by getting too friendly with Cameron.

"Dr. Powers? Now Ava, you know how we do," he said trying to lighten the mood by suggesting I didn't call him Dr. Powers anymore.

Sighing I decided to be completely blunt. "Listen Cameron, is that what you want me to call you? Why are you always coming up to me, speaking, laughing, joking, asking me how am I?" I sounded a bit irritated and I could tell he was taken aback.

"Do you see where we work?" he exclaimed spreading his arms out wide sporting that sexy ass smile of his. "You look a little upset is everything alright?" He asked in a more serious tone.

"Listen Dr… I mean Cameron I really have to go right now," I said cutting the conversation short.

"Well where are you going?" he asked.

Damn he was nosey and he was starting to work my nerves. I didn't want to tell him I needed to go get a restraining order against my crazy ass baby daddy who I almost killed the night before. I did what felt natural I became defensive.

"It's my day off," I said in a slightly hostile tone. "That means it's none of your business."

This man still didn't let up. If anything he became more persistent. Had it been any other day and had he not been married I'd humor myself and flirt a little but now was not the time and I definitely wasn't about to welcome him to run his hands over my face or my behind because he was being nice. Matter of fact how nice could he be standing out here tracking me down when he had a wife at home.

"Whoa," he said holding his hands up in the air. "Listen, we are friends you seem a little on edge and I thought maybe I could take you out to lunch get your mind off whatever it is that is bothering you." He stated sincerely.

"Contrary to what you might believe I don't need your sympathy," I spat. "And I'd appreciate it if you'd let me be on my way I don't have time for this."

I could tell I'd hurt his feelings but at that point I didn't give a damn everyone was a suspect. That's what men did they wooed you into believing they were heaven sent and then showed their true colors. I wasn't falling for the okie doke anymore. These niggas could kiss my little hot red ass.

"Look, I am sorry I bothered you," he said sounding a bit defeated. "Do you need me to take a look at your eyes?" He asked squinting trying to move in closer.

Instantly I became angry. Nosey ass just wanted to find out what happened. "I had a car accident!" I stated defensively.

I watched him as he looked at my car. Walked completely around it examining every inch of it as if he knew I was lying. He didn't even respond he just grunted which made me angrier. Okay so maybe I shouldn't have been angry but he wasn't anyone of importance to me and I didn't have to explain a damn thing to him or anyone else.

"I didn't ask you how you got those black eyes Ava," he said with sorrow in his voice. "Here," he said handing me my glasses. "Put these glasses back on you don't want those hens in there talking about you." With that he turned to walk away.

I felt like an ass. Cameron had always been so sweet to me. However, he was married maybe in another lifetime someone as good as him would have married me. If I was ever reincarnated I'd have a chance to live a beautiful life, a normal life and not have this dark cloud constantly lingering over my head. I wanted to call after him and tell him thank you but my pride wouldn't let me say a word.

I sat in my car watching him walk back inside the building wondering why I acted the way I did when my circumstances weren't any one's fault but my own. Why in the hell was I mad at him? He didn't do anything to me but try to be nice.

I drove slowly to my sister's office to find out how to go about stripping Rodney of all his parental rights. That man was clearly a danger to himself and to others. I needed to get the situation under control as quickly as possible.

I was so glad I made it to her office when I did she was just getting ready to leave for lunch. She told me she was meeting up with a friend of hers but didn't mind if I joined them. I chose to go handle my business by getting a restraining order and going home to get some rest. I was emotionally, mentally, and physically drained.

When I walked through my front door the potency hit me directly in my face. I shook my head confused as to what was going on. Now I knew it couldn't have been weed that I smelled. I knew Rodney hadn't gotten out of jail and brought his ass back up in my house. Was he even in jail yet or was he still laid up at the hospital recovering from that ass whipping I gave him? I followed the scent up the stairs and right to Dominique's door.

I could see the thick layers of smoke ascending from underneath her door and prayed that my eyes and nose were deceiving me. I opened the door to find her in a bra and panties and this little boy with dreads laying back on her bed in his boxers blowing smoke into the air.

"WHAT THE FUCK!!!!" I yelled at the top of my lungs startling both of them. Another day in the life of Ava Tanner straight fucked up.

# CAMERON

## (3)

I couldn't take my mind off Ava she was off work for the next four days but I kept wondering what she was doing. I wanted to know that she was safe. We had worked together for a very long time. It was no secret that her husband or whoever he was put his hands on her. I don't know how many times she'd come to work with some lame ass story talking about she fell down the stairs or had some type of accident. I was a medical professional I knew the signs of domestic violence when I saw them.

I can remember telling her about our EAP benefits and she flew off the handle like I was the one who had busted her lip and blacked her eyes. Everybody in the department talked about her except me. My colleague Perry really had a thing for her. At times I couldn't tell if he wanted to fuck her or slap her up too. The way his eyes burned holes through her every time he looked at her made me question who he was when he wasn't playing the role of medical professional.

She was a fine woman she had this skin tone that had a red tint to it she looked like she could be Indian. Her hair was long, thick, and dark. Her eyes were shaped like almonds a beautiful brown and warm. I loved working with her watching how attentive and caring she was with her patients. I'd make conversation with her just so I could keep her around me for a few more seconds than would otherwise be allotted considering we worked in a very busy atmosphere. Everything about her was amazing.

I'd never acted upon my attraction to her before because she was involved with someone and I was married not to mention we were coworkers. I didn't need any gossip floating around the department about me and one of the nurses but then again I'd never been one who cared about what other people had to say about me. Considering I was divorcing my wife of nine years I was aiming closer to taking a chance at pursuing her. Things just weren't working with Marteen and me. The longer I stayed with her the more I couldn't stand her. I used to look into her gray eyes and get lost in them now they looked like the eyes of the devil.

Marteen was crazy to put lightly. I'm not just saying that because it's over either. I should have seen the signs that she wasn't wrapped too tight when we first got together but I chose to ignore them because she was fine and had a fat ass to match. She was smart, witty, and sophisticated even when we were in college. Plus she saw in me at the time what I didn't see in myself. She gave me more confidence than I'd ever had. She was constantly pushing me to do better and when I went to medical school she had my back all the way. Well at least that's how things appeared to be.

You see Marteen was an opportunist. Any opportunity she saw to advance her standing in society she was on it. She didn't care who she crossed to get her position or keep it. When it came to getting her way Marteen was willing to go through hell or high water to reach her goal. There were never really any goals she had that were worth reaching though. She wanted a husband of status who made lots of money. She got me. She wanted picture perfect children and talked me into going to a fertility doctor and allowing her to undergo in vitro fertilization including a procedure called pre-implantation genetic diagnosis.

Every genetic trait down to the eye color our daughter Yasmine possessed was pre-planned. Now that I look back at it I had to have been crazy as hell to let this woman have me interfering with God's plan. But I did and the result was our beautiful little girl. After having our daughter I started to realize that Marteen didn't even like children it was all for show.

Even after spending long hours in my practice and at the hospital I was getting up with our daughter all times of night. I played with her, I nurtured her, I cared for her I loved that little girl with every fiber in my being. Marteen was more interested in going out to have drinks with her friends if that's what she wanted to call them so she could show off her new shoes or $2500 handbag. She'd even packed up and went out of town without telling me anything for eight days talking about she needed a break.

A break from what? She didn't do shit but spend my money trying to look good in the eyes of everyone else. She'd gotten ass implants with my money; Botox treatments, breast lifts, and anything else fake with MY MONEY! She didn't cook, she didn't clean, the only thing she could do was fuck me good and that was only when she wanted something extravagant.

Marteen was selfish and if the world didn't revolve around her it shouldn't revolve at all. I honestly had come to the conclusion she didn't have a caring bone in her body and that was why I wanted a divorce. I moved out of our plush home in a gated community into a condo a friend of mine owned. I was done with her for good. Our daughter? Now that was another story I'd always be a part of her life no matter what her mother did to keep me out of it. She was still trying to control me by using our daughter. If I didn't do what she thought I should when she thought I should do it she acted a fool.

I knew she wouldn't go away quietly. What should have been an easy process turned into something ugly. Even though she didn't deserve as much I was willing to give her the house, alimony, child support and enough of it to keep up the lifestyle she had become accustomed to. It wasn't enough for her she wanted me too. She couldn't stand the fact that I had decided to leave her she thought she was God's gift to not just men but mankind.

Sure I could be an asshole and put all of her dirty little secrets out in the open for everyone and their mama to know about the so called high class Marteen LeBlanc but for what? I'm not into mudslinging. However, she was making it more difficult than ever to act like an adult when dealing with her.

I stared at my daughter as she lay asleep in the middle of the living room floor. She was so beautiful a spitting image of her mother. She had those same gray eyes but soft and innocent. What I had wanted to be a Sunday afternoon with my daughter turned into a Sunday night with her falling asleep right after dinner. I shook my head in disgust there was always an excuse as to why she couldn't bring my daughter to me on time.

I was taken from my thoughts by a soft rapping on my front door. Glancing at my watch it was well past visiting time midnight to be exact. I got up from the couch and approached my door staring out through the peephole. It was my soon to be ex-wife. I opened the door slightly.

"Is that any way to greet your wife Cameron," she asked with a twirl of her long curly hair. Taking a quick look back at Yasmine I slid between the small crack in the door and greeted her outside. Standing there like a knight guarding the kings castle. I asked, "What are you doing here Marteen?" In a low non interested tone.

Still smiling and twirling her hair around her finger she looked me directly in my eyes, "What do you think I'm doing here?" she asked seductively.

I knew this was coming. I shook my head and turned to go back inside the house but she grabbed hold of my wife beater tugging to pull me back slowly but deliberately. "Can you just let me in for a minute," she whispered softly. "I just want to talk to you," she added.

Despite my better judgment I opened the door wider for her to come inside.

"Do you want something to drink?" I asked heading for the kitchen. I needed Vodka for whatever it was she was about to spring on me. Marteen had a way of fucking up a man's night and I was prepared for whatever it was she had to bring my way.

"Sure," she said. "My usual."

I didn't respond just continued toward the kitchen area. I pulled the glasses out of the cabinet jumping sending the glass crashing to the floor when I turned to see her standing before me. They shattered into tiny pieces. As Marteen walked closer to me I could hear the glass crunching under her heels. She took slow seductive steps swaying her hips. Her stomach was flat, breast perky; her plump pussy was shaved and smooth, looking just right. I closed my eyes in an effort to erase her from my mind. I could feel her press up against me my tool poking her in the stomach.

"See there," she said tugging at my sweat pants. "I knew you missed me."

My big head was screaming no but I couldn't stop my little head from responding. I couldn't resist her or maybe it had been so long I just didn't want to resist her. I allowed her to pull my hardness from my pants and watched her slide down my body to take me into her mouth. I closed my eyes listening to the slurping and moaning sounds she made as she wet me up with her mouth.

I was hard as a rock. I grabbed the back of her head and pushed myself deeper inside of her hitting the back of her throat. She gagged and moaned never pulling away taking all nine inches of me inside. She grabbed my ass and pulled me further into her never missing a beat matching my rhythm I felt myself about to come. My body tensed up. Damn I didn't want to nut that fast but Marteen was doing her thang.

"I'm about to cum," I whispered in a low raspy voice. She sucked harder twirling her tongue on my dick, moaning, slurping, as saliva dripped down her chin. When it was all said and done I was squirting down her throat and she was swallowing everything had given her.

I wanted more. For a minute she had managed to take me back to a time when we were happy. I snatched her up sat her on the counter and entered her slowly. She was so warm, wet; tight I stood there for a minute enjoying being inside of her. My tongue teasing her nipples I knew that was what she liked I could feel her becoming wetter with every stroke of my tongue I began to thrust myself in and out of her.

She was sitting on my countertop legs over my shoulders as I pounded her. Damn her pussy felt so good. We moaned together as I went deeper hitting her g spot causing her moans to turn into faint whimpers.

"Mmmmm Ava damn," I slurred as I started to cum again.

Her rhythm stopped as she lifted my head up looking at me like I was crazy.

"Who the fuck did you just call me?" She asked with authority. Honestly at the time I didn't know what the hell she was talking about.

"Marteen," I said with a confused look on my face.

"No the fuck you didn't. You called me Ava," she responded looking like she wanted to knock the hell out of me. She slid my dick out of her and hopped off the cabinet. "Are you serious Cameron?" She yelled. I tried to quiet her down Yasmine was in the other room sleep. I shouldn't have let her in let alone fucked her. "You're calling me some bitches fucking name!" She yelled even louder.

I quickly pulled up my pants looking back making sure Yasmine hadn't heard the commotion in the kitchen.

"Marteen our daughter is asleep in the other room," I whispered with an irritated look on my face.

"So what!" She screamed. "She will be up in a minute anyway," she said putting her clothes back on. "I'm taking her home. She's not staying over here around you and your little girlfriend. I am your damn wife!"

"It's late Marteen and she is sleep I will bring her home in the morning," I said exasperated from all her drama and coming twice in less than thirty minutes.

We went back and forth for the next couple of minutes until I finally gave up. I just wanted her ass out of my house and fast. I never asked her ass to come over I never told her I wanted her pussy. Maybe I did call her Ava how else would she come up with the name? But hell it was over between Marteen and I. There was nothing left to be said maybe this was enough to keep her ass off my doorstep in the middle of the night.

Sure I was a little remorseful for calling her another woman's name but that didn't hold a candle to things she had done to me during our marriage. Maybe she got exactly what she deserved. Her feelings hurt if she had any. I followed her into the living room where she quietly picked up our daughter and headed towards the door.

Watching her on her little triade I could see how a man could hit a woman. At times she made me want to knock her head off. My mama taught me better than that though. I would handle her the correct way and remember to keep my dick in my pants. I didn't say a word as she stormed out the house cursing under her breath the entire time. I was thankful my daughter hadn't awakened to witness a mother having another one of her fits.

I stood in the doorway to make sure she got in her car safely and slammed the door. Looking down at my dick I shook my head. I was smarter than that it had been seven months since I'd slept with her and there I was back tracking. I heard my phone whistling signaling I had a text message. *I hope you got a damn good look at your daughter because you will never see her again you fucking bastard.* I didn't even respond I would talk to Marteen when she calmed down.

The way she was now there was no point in trying to reason with her. When she was mad that was that there was no getting around it until she was finished throwing her little hissy fit. Childish is the only word that can describe it. What did our daughter have to do with me calling her another woman's name when we were having sex? Not a damn thing. Yes we were technically still married but I wasn't with her I wasn't with Ava either but that was none of her damn business I didn't have to explain shit to that woman.

That woman had a way of taking me out of my element every single time. I should have just left her ass a long time ago. But I didn't. Thought she was too fine for me to let go. When she cheated the first time because I worked too much I forgave her. When she cheated the second time because I wasn't showing her enough attention I forgave her. But that last time I caught her cheating I couldn't let that go it was time to leave. It was like a baseball game three strikes and your ass is out. I deserved better or I would just be alone simple as that. There was no way she was going to finesse me into thinking that shit was my fault.

# LAUREN

## (4)

I couldn't believe my parents had kept me in the dark for so long about my father's health. I mean sure they didn't want me to worry but prostate cancer. When the hell were they going to tell me? When he died? I had actually said that to my mother and I thought she was going to come through the phone on my ass. At that point it didn't matter to me he was my father and I loved him deeply. There was no reason for them to try to keep secrets. I could have been doing something even if it only meant spending more time. Time I could never get back.

I guess it was water under the bridge at that point but I was still pissed. They were up to their necks in medical debt trying to pay for daddy's treatments when they could have just come to me. Yeah I know I was working a mediocre job with mediocre pay but I could've been doing what I started doing when I found out my parents were having trouble paying for daddy's medical bills and to keep food in the fridge, the electricity on, water running and everything else.

There was nothing I wouldn't do to make sure daddy was alright. I knew they were on a fixed income but I didn't know they were doing so badly. I could remember a time when mama and daddy both worked and daddy was bringing in damn near 90k a year at the tire plant. They were never hurting for money but now things had changed. The casino took a lot of their money and they were living paycheck to paycheck.

It didn't take much for me to make my decision I was a good looking woman although I was in my thirties young men always approached me thinking I was in my early twenties. "You don't look that old," is what they would say when I shot them down real lady like and told them I was a grown woman. I didn't know if that was a compliment or not. Hell I am not old I am seasoned!

I walked right into the upscale strip club in my tallest boots my skimpiest outfit and put on a show they were sure to remember. My long silky legs wrapping around that pole, my chocolate ass cheeks clapping to the bass, my award winning smile and my Bohemian hair flowing like it was all mine caught the attention of every man and woman watching. You would've thought I'd been doing this thang for years courtesy of the pole dancing workout classes I prided myself in taking. They say everything happens for a reason this reason being helping improve daddy's quality of life.

With the extra money I was making I was able to pay all of my parents' bills and do some extra shopping for myself. Every mall within a 200 mile radius was now my best friend. I was seriously thinking about quitting my day job. Yeah so what I was in my mid 30's there were 20 year olds that couldn't fuck with me in the looks department. Shiiitttt and my knees were still good. The things eating right and taking care of your body would do for you. I didn't have any stretch marks or any kids to hold me back.

I was working every night Tuesday through Saturday bringing in a stack on a bad night. All the bitches in the club were hating wanting to know where I was from. They didn't need to know all that. All they needed to know was I was there and I took their clients at will. I was monopolizing in that bitch and it wasn't shit they were going to do about. I was a bad bitch everything they wanted to be. If they had a problem with it they could take it up with the owner and I knew he wasn't letting me go for damn sure. I came in running and I was making him far too much cash. If they were mad they could go find another club to work in because I had that particular spot sewed up.

I smirked as I walked through the mall carrying two handfuls of bags. Popping tags had become my favorite hobby. I walked inside my favorite shoe store and started trying on one pair of shoes after another. It was an expensive place to shop and I didn't quite have it like that well at least not yet but I was definitely going to be buying at least two pairs.

When I walked up to the counter to pay for my shoes the sales associate handed me several bags. I looked at her like she was crazy. I was about to cop an attitude until she opened her mouth and spoke the words of angels.

"These are paid for," she said smiling. I quickly totaled up the merchandise in my head. Yeah she was happy her ass was getting a fat ass commission check. I looked around but didn't see anyone. I was so enthralled in trying on shoes I hadn't even noticed anyone else come into the store.

"Who paid for these?" I asked feeling a little paranoid. Maybe it was one of the tricks from the club. I damn sure wasn't too happy about running into one those bastards during my off time. Sometimes they could get downright ignorant. I prided myself in not being bourgeois and being about my money and my money only. It was a job and sometimes you had to take a little abuse to get that paper.

"I'm not sure where he went miss," the lady said still grinning from ear to ear. "But I am sure he will make himself known soon," she added winking.

I didn't want to look over my shoulder for the rest of my day so I opted to head out to the car and leave. Although I was happy about the gifts I damn sure didn't want anyone stalking me trying to follow me home and shit. That would be a problem.

Going with Ava to take those shooting lessons and purchasing a gun was a good move after all. If anyone ran up on me on some bullshit he definitely wouldn't be leaving the way he came. When I finally reached my car I popped open the trunk and began loading the bags inside still looking over my shoulder not sure what to expect. Sure it was a nice gesture but believe me everything came with a price. People just didn't do shit for free these days. Some prices I wasn't willing to pay or should I say I didn't want anyone forcing me to pay them.

"Excuse me miss," I heard someone say as I was about to get into my car. I slid my hand into my Hermes bag and put my finger around the trigger. My nine was cocked and loaded.

I was looking at one of the finest and I mean FINEST brothers I had ever laid eyes on in my life. 6'4" about 170lbs body looking tight and right even up underneath his clothes. I couldn't let him know he made me cream my panties so I played it cool eyeing him like he was bothering me.

"Can I help you?" I asked with a lot of attitude.

"Do you have a minute?" he asked smiling.

"Listen," I started rolling my eyes in my head. "You're going to have to make this real quick because I have things to do." I huffed. Okay so I was laying on the attitude a little too thick. The fact is I'm grown and I can do whatever I want to do. He could like it or leave it.

"Okay," he said grinning trailing his beard with his fingers. "My names Dollar and uh I was wondering why your man let you come out the house by yourself."

I chuckled shaking my head why couldn't these men just say what they mean and mean what they said? Seriously was that the only lame ass line they could come up with these days? I'd heard that same question time and time again. Honestly as cool as they must have thought they sounded it was by far the dumbest way to ask a woman if she had a man.

"Is that your way of asking me if I have a man?" I responded staring him directly in his eyes.

Probably realizing he was making a fool out of himself he tilted his head to the side smiling showing the deepest set of dimples I'd ever seen and answered, "As a matter of fact Dollar was."

I stood there for a moment pondering what I was going to say next. The truth of the matter was I hadn't had a man in years. Well not a man of my own. I didn't have time for a man I was trying to get me right and they didn't cause anything but problems. And I sure as hell didn't have that to do. I talked a lot of shit but I wasn't going to bust a grape in a fruit fight anyone who knew me knew that. That's why my girls Ava and Brooke always had to come rushing to my rescue. I stayed writing checks my ass couldn't cash but it never stopped me from talking shit.

"As a matter of fact I don't," I responded sliding my tongue over my teeth with a slight grin.

I could tell the brotha thought his Mack game was strong because I noticed his chest swelling up and he got a little more confidence as he stepped in on me invading my personal space and backing me up against my car.

"In that case," he said speaking directly in my ear. "Why don't you give Dollar your number?" He responded pulling out his cell phone.

Okay was I tripping or was the nigga continuing to refer to himself as if he was not himself? Normally I would have been turned the hell off but something about the way he looked at me, his voice, the way his lips moved when he spoke had me all hot and bothered. His cockiness was apparent but if you people don't know me by now you better ask somebody he wasn't about to get off that easy. At least not with my sexy ass because as fine as he was I was finer and I had the world in between my legs which meant there was nothing in this world I couldn't get.

"Unfortunately...... Um what did you say your name was again?" I asked with a confused look on my face. That must of threw him for a loop because he backed up off me a little bit which was cool because I learned never to let them see you coming. You control the situation that way. I knew how to play my position act like he didn't matter and pretend as if I wasn't sweating the fact that he was sweating me.

"Dollar," he responded losing some of confidence and flaring his nose. Was that anger I sensed? Oh hell no I didn't get down with violent men I don't care how fine they were. I could read these niggas like a student reads a textbook. Wasn't nan nigga putting his hands on me. Any man who got mad because I wasn't going to let him choose could kiss my ass! I did the choosing could kiss my ass. Which meant this guy wasn't the dude for me.

Still continuing on my little charade I eyed him closely, "Well Dollar," I let his name roll off my tongue this time invading his personal space and letting my lips slightly touch his neck. "Why don't you give me your number and I'll call you." I said bringing my voice up an octane or two and giving him almost fifty feet.

I thoroughly enjoyed playing these little games with men. They were so predictable and stupid. His arrogance got his ass played. I wasn't calling him for what? Maybe on a night when I was bored which as of lately was NEVER. I wasn't stupid enough to let his fine ass get me in closed quarters hell I just might be bamboozled into giving him some.

Smiling I pulled my phone from my Hermes bag handing it to him and looking at him impatiently.

"So this is how you gon' treat Dollar after he just bought you eight pairs of shoes?" he asked with a smirk on his face. It was cool that he had just spent several thousand dollars on a perfect stranger which just so happened to be me but from the looks of things he was a nigga that got money quickly anyway so he wasn't losing. Shit like that was the norm for him.

There he went with that Dollar shit "So you're the stalker who goes around spying on the pretty ladies trying on shoes?" I asked meeting his wit with a little of my own.

He just laughed shaking his head as he put his number in my phone. "Make sure you put your real name in there," I said just because I could and I hated nicknames anyway.

"Only if you really intend on calling," he said not looking up from my phone.

"I guess that is something we will have to find out huh?" I asked as he handed me my phone. Slipping into my car I started the engine and made my exit. He stood outside my car I guess he was waiting on a goodbye. Well he wasn't getting one I had already wasted too much time shooting the shit with him about nothing. I quickly backed out of my parking space and bent the corner looking in my rear view mirror. He was standing there with his hands in the air like what's up. Laughing I honked my horn and sped off thinking how good some of us really had it.

Picking up my phone I looked at my new contact. *Dollar.* Clearly "Dollar" didn't want me to call because he couldn't follow instructions. DELETE CONTACT. I had to get home it was time to get ready to head into work it was the weekend. Which meant it was time to get money after all that was what made the world go around.

Driving I noticed a black car with dark tinted windows behind me. At first I didn't think anything of it until I made a right then a left and the car was still behind me. I might have been spooking myself but I wasn't taking any chances. In the past couple months I had stepped on plenty toes. I was going to have to pay the piper but today just wasn't that today.

I bent a couple more corners and looked back again. Damn this car was still on my ass. I picked up my phone and called Brooke told her to meet me at the spot. I pulled into the projects parked my car in front of the house with twenty niggas standing outside and got out. It kept rolling. Maybe I was overreacting but I'd rather be safe than sorry. I walked up to Chaz getting welcomed with a big hug. Damn I loved Brooke's brothers. Especially Chaz he had a thing for me when we were kids nothing ever became of it but it was always good to know

I had him in my corner. He was a big man did a stint or two well maybe three in the penitentiary but that didn't stop him from stacking paper and handling his business. He was a street legend and although I'd never given him any I was his baby.

"Sup lil mama? You good?" He asked eyeing the black car hard.

I felt a chill run up my spine I was nervous as hell but as opposed to telling him someone was following me I smiled and said things were cool. He didn't take his eyes off the car until it was out seeing distance. He looked down at me as I shrugged my shoulders. From the smirk on his face I knew that he could tell I was lying.

"Let me find out you done got yourself in some shit. You gon' make me have to kill a nigga," he said not cracking a smile.

That's why I loved me some Chaz. He was that dude and I always felt safe around him. I had never seen him lose his temper except once and it wasn't nothing nice. I'd heard he put a couple people to sleep in his lifetime but you know that was just hearsay on the streets. Sometimes you could believe it sometimes stories were fabricated. I'll let you be the judge.

Brooke pulled into the parking stall right next to mine bringing her car into a screeching halt. She jumped out looking crazy as hell.

"What's going on sis?" She asked looking like she was ready fight. I just laughed she was younger than me I had taken a liking to her seeing her around the neighborhood. For some reason we clicked and I always saw her as my baby sister. I guess you could say I was her little big sister because she was always trying to take up for me like she was the eldest.

I laughed. "Girl nothing," I lied. "I just wanted to be with the fam before I headed home," I said lying again. I was going to have to stop that shit but I couldn't tell them I was stripping even if it was because my daddy was sick that was going to remain a secret. I wouldn't hear the end of that shit. I didn't feel like defending myself and I didn't want to stop so for the time being I would keep it to myself. At least until the shit hit the fan and I didn't have a choice but to come clean.

# MARTEEN

## (5)

I was still pissed as I drove down the highway headed towards having lunch with my best friend Ashley. I hadn't spoken with Cameron in almost two weeks didn't answer his calls and wasn't about to let him see Yasmine. After all we'd been through together he was divorcing me and calling me some whore's name? Pissed wasn't even the word I was livid. He thought he had seen my bad side he just didn't know what he was up against.

Why was it I could manage to get him to make love to me but I couldn't keep him interested in me? What did this Ava person have that I didn't? After all he did say I do to me and had a child with me. I had that baby for him I didn't even want kids but he talked me into bearing his child. That part is working out in my favor but who wants to be a mother when they can be free? I loved the little girl but I didn't want to be around her all the time.

I tried to be a good mother but I just didn't feel connected to her. She looked exactly like me but she had come in between my husband and I. Ever since we had that baby he catered to her every need and just left me to the side like I was a piece of trash. That was the only reason I'd started cheating on him, spending his money frivolously when he told me not to and lying about it all. It was to protect our relationship it was to save our marriage. Without the other men or my little shopping sprees it would have all fallen apart. I would have fallen apart.

Fuck! Why couldn't he see that I loved him more than anything in the world? Or maybe he could see but just didn't care. Maybe Ava was getting all his attention now maybe. She had to have been why he asked for a divorce. He had fallen in love with another woman. I slammed my hand against the steering wheel screaming out obscenities wishing he were standing in front of my BMW so I could run his cheating ass over. Yes I cheated but it was to make our marriage better.

I blinked away the tears that were welling up in my eyes and checked in the mirror to make sure I didn't look a mess before I met up with Ashley. I was going so fast I lost control of the wheel swerving and struggling to regain control while Yasmine began screaming and crying in the background. Would she just shut the fuck up? This kid was always crying about something. I looked in the rearview mirror again at her red tear stained face and frowned.

"Quiet down honey," I said in the sweetest voice I could muster. I was trying to keep myself calm. It was times like this when she interrupted my thoughts that made me want to smother her with a pillow. I am sure mommy and daddy wouldn't condone that. That's what I felt though. I'd smother her father too if he didn't come back home soon. I couldn't count how many times my parents had gotten me out of situations where I lost my temper. As I've grown I've gotten better with that issue but it didn't stop the thoughts from coming.

Cameron had always kept me grounded. He loved me for me and never once held anything against me. If I wanted something he made sure I had it. We never had any problems at least not until recently. The voices in my head were coming more frequently and I felt like my life was spinning out of control without him by my side. I couldn't live without him and he couldn't live without me. I wouldn't allow that ever. I just had to find out who was coming in between us and get rid of her.

My cell phone rang glancing at the caller id I hit ignore. I was not answering that phone call. The more I ignored the calls the more he would dial my number until I answered it. I wasn't about to entertain any conversation with him he was the reason my marriage was in shambles if he would have just kept his ass away from me I would have never slept with him. Oh no he couldn't do that he had to keep on fucking with me!

I'd been so lost in my own thoughts and missed my exit. Making a sharp right I skid off the highway and it would be my luck a cop started blaring his sirens behind me. Rolling my eyes in the back of my head I slowly pulled over took out my license and registration and waited for the pig to approach my car.

I hated cops but I knew how to work them. All of them were suckers for a pretty face and a couple ear tickling words. I'd get out of a ticket and be on my way. Looking back at Yasmine I noticed she had cried herself to sleep. *Good.* I thought. I was tired of hearing her whine about nothing at all. Giving myself the once over I rolled down my window just as the officer approached the car. I squinted trying to look up at the officer but the sun blinded my vision.

"Marteen?" the officer asked.

I strained to see what damn police officer knew me on a first name basis. I prayed it wasn't someone I'd had a run in with during my younger days because I definitely wouldn't be able to flirt my way out of a ticket today.

"Marteen Leblanc," his country drawl was evident that time. I knew exactly who was standing next to my window, Chester Bloomfield. Country bumpkin ass negroe. Laughing to myself I nodded my head in agreement yes it was me Marteen Leblanc-Powers.

"Chester Bloomfield?" I responded pretending to be excited. I ran circles around that country ass negroe back in high school and for a little while in college. He had the biggest crush on me. I had him chasing me around like a little lost puppy dog. He was going to the NFL and promised to make me a very happy and rich woman but then he got injured and well let's just say that injury hurt our little love affair too.

"It's been a long time since I seen you gul," he said in his southern drawl. I cringed every time he spoke. He had to be one of the dumbest people on the planet. How in the hell did he get on the police force? Didn't they have to take some kind of written test? Things probably hadn't changed much since our school days I was sure he'd cheated his way through that damn test because he sure as hell couldn't have passed it on his own.

"I know! How have you been?" I asked pretending to be excited to see him.

"Ow well you know," he said standing back so I could take a look at him in his tight ass uniform. "I'm a officer of de law," he said.

*Oh my God* I screamed inside my head. This man was still a complete idiot hadn't evolved at all. Dumb as a bag of rocks. I remember the day I dumped his simple behind. He cried like a baby begged me to stay. I wasn't having it at all. No contract no love. What can I say? Money was my best friend, my lover, my confidant, it made me come.

"Hmmm I see," I responded giving him the once over as if I was truly interested in him being a broke ass *"officer of de law"*.

"I'll be damned I haven't seent you in a spell bootiful Miss Lady," he said looking in the backseat noticing Yasmine asleep. "Is that your lil' bebe?" he asked.

I nodded my head in agreement and plastered the fakest smile I could muster. "Yes, that is my daughter," I responded.

"You should be mo' careful drivin' wouldn't won't you lil gals to get into no accident," he said trailing his eyes from mine down to my empty ring finger.

I didn't have on my ring not because I didn't want to have it on but because it had somehow mysteriously disappeared when Cameron left. He always thought he could outsmart me but I was getting that ring back and him. He was the love of my life.

"I heard you were married to some big time doctor," he said still staring at my ring finger.

"You know how things go in this day and age," I responded sadly. "We are currently separated. I just need a little break." I lied.

"Can I take you out sometimes?" he asked with a huge smile on his face until he noticed the look I was giving him.

"Uh uh you know until that there you were telling me about is over." He added quickly.

Inside my mind I was screaming no but what rolled off my tongue even surprised me. "Sure why not Mr. Bloomfield," I said with a smile. He could be of good use to me. I wasn't a tramp or anything but I had to be honest with myself I was not getting any on a regular basis and Chester would be a good candidate to keep me company while I worked on mending things with my husband. Not to mention he was packing a little something in between those thighs.

The sex with Chester had always been great even when we were kids. I could remember riding him as my eyes were closed so I wouldn't have to look at the dumb ass expressions he made. Every time he tried to talk I would do something to shut him back up. I didn't want his stupid ass making any noise interrupting my groove. He would have been an okay guy if he never had to speak. All he had to do was stand there looking sexy and never and I mean never utter a word because once he opened his mouth the fantasy would be over.

He took out his notepad as I gave him my telephone number wondering if I was making the right decision. Even if I was going to regret it in the future he would serve his purpose for the time being. I took his number as well listing it in my phone as Chelsea just in case Cam ever decided to go through my phone. He'd done so before. Well he'd done so the day he left when he walked in on me having hot sweaty sex in our bed with his brother.

I tried to explain that it wasn't my fault it was his brothers'. He had a way with the ladies. He could talk a nun out of her panties. I always knew he wanted me just by the way he used to look at me with those sneaky ass eyes. He would undress me visually every time he saw me and he was sexy as fuck I would do the same but I didn't tell him to come over and seduce me.

He strolled up in our house like he owned the place. Snatching me up and pounding me until my knees were weak. I wanted to say stop but every time I opened my mouth all I could do was moan or tell him not to stop. He was the total opposite of his brother. While his brother was gentle and loving he was rough, raw, and animalistic even. He didn't have a care in the world being with a man who didn't have any regrets or make any excuses made my body in particular my pie speak languages I didn't know it could speak. He was not marriage material but he was fucking material all day.

He wouldn't be able to give me the things that Cameron did. He wasn't professional he didn't meet the standards to be called my man. That day I begged and pleaded for Cameron to stay. I even fought him to keep him from leaving but he still walked out the door. He didn't believe that this time it wasn't my fault. Said I was always gapping my legs open for some other nigga. I had never heard my husband speak that way. I guess you could take the man out the ghetto but you couldn't take the ghetto out of the man.

He packed his things and never stepped a foot back into our home. Within twenty four hours he had divorced papers delivered to our home. 24 hours! I know he didn't think he was getting rid of me that easily. I would fight him tooth and nail. I didn't want him to leave me I loved him more than air. I'd even take it back if I could. I tried to talk to him but he said that was my M.O. he knew he had married a gold diggin' ass hoe but didn't want to believe it. Thought I would change for him.

Marteen LeBlanc was not anyone's whore. I was just misunderstood. He was my husband he was supposed to be there for me all the time. He should have been there to keep his brother from trying to rape me. Yeah I went there I told him that his older brother Kymani forced himself on me. Do you know he had the nerve to look at me and shake his head like he was disappointed in me? He didn't believe me. I didn't ask for that. Alright so I participated once it got started but that still made me the victim.

I never asked for any of that. I didn't ask for him to work all the time, I didn't ask for him to be tired all the time, I didn't ask for the kid I had sitting in the backseat. The only thing I did get that I asked for was a husband on paper. He wasn't holding up his end of the bargain I was his wife. I made sure the cleaning service kept the house up, I made sure the nanny took very good care of our daughter, and I made sure there was someone to cook dinner every single day so he would never be hungry.

He had the nerve to complain about my spending habits. Didn't he understand how hard it was to take care of a household? Of course he didn't because he was too busy at that damn hospital doing God knows what. I wasn't a fool by a long shot he was either cheating with someone at that hospital or he wasn't at the hospital when he said he was. Marteen LeBlanc would definitely find out though and maybe Chester, now that I'd found him again being a police officer and all could help me out.

It wouldn't hurt anything for him to help me. All I needed was information it wasn't like I was trying to interfere in some kind of police investigation. I know I said he was dumb but I was sure there was something in that pea brain of his that could be useful to me. After all he had helped me with that one thing so many years ago. I guess there were a couple things that Chester was good for. I smiled bigger on the outside and I guess he took that as his queue to continue to speak.

"Marteen," he started.

Cutting him off I said, "Listen, I have somewhere to be right now and I know you need to get back to work so call me," I said putting my car in drive and speeding off leaving his simple ass behind. Looking down at my vibrating phone I read the text. *Slow down!* Shaking my head I kept driving didn't this damn idiot know texting and driving was probably more dangerous than my speeding?

I pulled up to the quaint little café about ten minutes later. Rushing in I sat down at the table next to Ashley pretending to be out of breath. Really I could care less about being late for our lunch the best always comes last. I would never tell her that because she was the attorney on my divorce case and I needed her 100% for me.

"Fashionably late as always," she responded not looking up from her menu.

Sometimes I thought she said things just to get up under my skin. Why did she even have to say anything other than maybe, "hello friend" or "it's nice to see you friend" or "I'm so happy you are here friend". She was my lawyer but I was paying her high sadity thinking she is better than everybody ass good money. She wasn't better than anybody she had to go to work every day to afford those Christian Louboutin's all I had to do was look pretty.

She had to bust her ass every day for someone else. I paid help. Yes help like her. I was better than her and she'd better get that straight before she found her ass standing in the unemployment line. She was nothing special lawyers came a dime a dozen in this town and the only reason I went to her is so she could make some money.

I wasn't sure what her business was like and I didn't really give a damn but what was going to happen is she was going to show me some respect. I didn't respond to little smart remark instead I signaled the waitress and ordered a mimosa.

"Where is Yasmine?" Ashley asked while taking a sip of her drink.

"She's with the nanny," I lied. Yasmine was in the car asleep. I didn't have the time, patience, or strength to lug her thirty pound body into the café in these heels. My windows were tinted dark enough and I had cracked them enough so she wouldn't be suffocated by the heat.

"You have the most beautiful daughter Marteen," she started. "That little girl is like a breath of fresh air." She said smiling.

I couldn't believe this jealous woman sitting before me. What was all this talk about my little girl? I don't know why she was so worried about Yasmine she needed to focus on getting a husband and a family of her own and stop worrying about mine. I could tell this was going to be a long lunch or at least in my mind because she was working my nerves already and I hadn't been seated but five minutes.

# AVA

## (6)

On the way to the little hole in the wall Brooke complained nonstop about how bad she was cramping and hated being on her rag. Yes she used exactly those words. It would definitely be a long night of waitressing for her.

"That'll be eight dollars," Brooke said for the second time. I could tell she was growing impatient with the patron inside the bar. The man pulled two more dollars out of his dingy pants pocket totaling six bucks. "EIGHT DOLLARS!" she repeated. The look on her face let me know she was ready to slap the hell out of him if he didn't quit playing games with her. I watched the entire scene play out like something in a movie.

The broke ass bastard sitting in front of her was causing her patience to wear thin and who knows what that crazy girl would do next. He held the money up higher shoving it towards her face. She smacked his hands away knocking the money to the ground before storming back to the bar.

She looked at the bartender yelling loud enough for the entire city to hear, "This nigga ain't got no damn money!" Her voice boomed even over the bass that was coming out of the speakers of the small club she'd been waitressing at for five years. She glared over at the drunken customer who had picked up his cash and was now holding it high in the air as if to say, *Bitch here's my six dollars for my eight dollar drink. Come get it because this nigga do got some money!*

She mouthed back at him *broke bitch* and turned her attention back to Stephanie the bartender. That had to have been the funniest exchange I'd ever witnessed in my life. I couldn't stop laughing as I strolled over to the bar to sit in front of the duo.

"Honey," Stephanie started in between laughter. "He wants you to come get his little $6.00." I was amazed at how this older woman always kept her cool in that crazy place. She was a smooth, laid back older lady with skin dark as coal and a small yellow afro. Her heavy build put a few years on her age wise and the nightlife hadn't done anything for her either but she was sweet. Everybody loved Ms. Stephanie and when we all needed some real advice she was our go to person. She was like our "other mom".

"Fuck his $6.00," Brooke spat. "I'm two seconds from shoving it down his damn throat. Or calling Chaz and Marcus over here to shut this place down for the night!" she added serious as a heart attack. Ms. Stephanie and I were doubled over in laughter. Anyone within earshot was enjoying the comedy that had unfolded. She however didn't see the humor in it and told us all fuck you before she tilted her head back and slammed a shot of Ciroc. "I guarantee I won't be serving his ass a damn thang tonight." She huffed.

He slowly stood swaying trying to keep his balance and began to stumble away eyeing her down. She glared right back at him until he was out of sight. She was most definitely a Johnson. I laughed as I thought about how her and both of her brothers blood boiled nonstop. They had good hearts though and they would do anything for the people they loved.

"I'll be back," Brooke told me as she strutted towards the bathroom. I looked at Ms. Stephanie and we fell out laughing again. I definitely needed to get out and have a drink or two my life had been in an uproar. I had a fast ass daughter, a crazy ass baby daddy, an asshole for a boss, and Cameron well he just wasn't taking no for an answer no matter how much I tried to avoid him.

I was doing good steering clear of him for a minute but eventually he caught up with me. He even apologized to me for what exactly I didn't know. He hadn't done anything wrong. Maybe it was for calling me a liar about my car accident without really coming out and calling me a liar. It could have been for asking me out on a date. Maybe he didn't want a sexual harassment suit against him. If he knew what Perry had done to me and what I was going through with him on a daily basis he wouldn't feel that way at all. I still hadn't uttered a word to anyone about that incident.

Why was I sitting there thinking about those things? I was supposed to be out having a good time with my girls. Speaking of girls I wondered why Lauren hadn't made it out with us. She was acting really secretive lately I wondered what was up with her. Knowing Lauren she was just being antisocial she got like that sometimes where she just liked to be in her own world. We all needed that "me" time so I understood. Brooke never could she loved being around us. She was like our little sister.

Speaking of the little sister she had been in the bathroom for quite some time. What did she do fall in the toilet? It was cool sitting at the bar talking to Stephanie but she was working hard mixing drinks and collecting tips. I slid off the barstool and headed to the bathroom. I walked in and found Brooke being who she always was exchanging heated words with another waitress, Tiara. I never understood why those two didn't get along. Maybe it was because from what I could see they acted just alike. But I wasn't going to question it and when it was time to ride I knew who I was going with.

I stood there standing next to the overflowing trash bin and the small dirty sink with the continuous drip. Sheets of toilet paper were strewn all over the wet floor. Some people were just nasty. Who left a bathroom looking like that? Yeah it's not your house and it's a small. Some would even call the establishment hood but damn! Really? You can at least pick up after yourself. I didn't touch a thing wasn't no telling what kind of nasty germs and bacteria were floating around in the two stall restroom.

"I think you heard me correctly," Brooke told the light skinned girl with the freckles rolling her eyes and sucking her teeth. I stood thinking this girl does not want to start with this little firecracker tonight.

"Brooke," I said snapping her glare in my direction. Um are her pupils dilated? I know she hasn't been in here getting high. Oh hell no I for damn sure was going to be getting to the bottom of this she knew better. "Let's get on back out here so you can finish off your shift." I said not even acknowledging Tiara standing there.

"Yeah," Tiara chimed in. "Listen to your friend and get your ass up outta here." She said waving her hand as if she was shooing someone away.

The look on Brookes face let me know that things were about to get physical. I couldn't let that happen. In yesteryear we used to get down a little bit. But we were grown ass women

54

now. Who in the hell wanted to be running around fighting people especially in nasty ass club bathrooms. Brooke's eyes told me she didn't give a fuck about being grown. The club was packed and it was warm in the dingy bathroom but she was sweating like a race horse.

Before I could even respond Brooke started swinging wildly. Bop bop bop right on top of Tiara's head knocking me and her challenger up against the trash bin and into the wall. I tried to maneuver my way around and grab my friend but she had Tiara pinned against me and I was stuck to the wall. I even took a couple shots that missed her opponent.

Damn she was messing up my buzz and my clothes. I mustered up all my strength and pushed Tiara and Brooke backwards charging Brooke and pushing her into one of the stalls. Tiara came charging but I stopped her in her tracks.

"I'm not about to be in here playing these little childish ass games with ya'll back the fuck up because if you hit me you gon' have two of us on yo ass up in here," I told her. That hood chick came up out of me quick. I didn't have time for any of this. I was pissed at Brooke and I was ready to go the hell home. Tiara thought better of running up on Brooke and exited but not before saying it wasn't over. Blah blah blah bitch get the fuck out was Brooke's response.

I stood there still holding my friend staring at her pissed. She was sweating and heaving, eyes dilated and wide open. She was clenching her jaws and I immediately became concerned. This girl was high on ecstasy. I took in a deep breath and exhaled slowly kicking the side of the stall. How long had she been doing this and why was it that no one had seen the signs?

So what everybody rapped about it in their songs poppin' molly's swallowing blue dolphins but fuck that. That shit was meth, heroin, cocaine, and fucking who knows what else. She knew better than that. We saw junkies running around our neighborhood all of our lives looking like straight zombies and here she was indulging in this bullshit.

"Brooke!" I yelled. She was overly alert and probably would have heard me if I whispered her name but I didn't give a damn. She sat there looking at me eyes wide open gritting her teeth with her nose flared like she was about to hit me too. Oh hell no she wasn't. I knew she probably felt like she could crush a mountain but it wasn't going down tonight. She wasn't working tonight I was taking her ass right on home and I was calling Chaz and telling on her little ass.

"This don't make no damn sense," I said snatching her up sounding like my mama.

"What?" she snapped at me. Her mood was crazy. I couldn't take it. I hated being around drug addicts. Yes even if she did it recreationally she was a drug addict, a junkie, a crack head, or whatever else they were called. I just said no to drugs well hard drugs. I could deal with her smoking a little weed but this shit was something else.

"I'm not even about to answer your stupid ass question!" I snapped back pulling her arm. She snatched away and gave me a look like *bitch don't put your hands on me like that.* "Oh so what you want to fight me too?" I said giving her a sideways look right back. This shit was for the birds I didn't have time to be babysitting this girl. I had my own damn problems and I needed to have my ass at home with my kids any damn way. I did just what I needed to do. I got ghost.

Instead of getting into an exchange with a drunk ass dope fiend I let her go slung my bag back over my shoulder and walked out shaking my head and leaving her ass standing there rolling and looking stupid. Wait until I told Lauren about this shit.

I hopped in my car and took a quiet ride home. I'd babysat my drink all night long so I wasn't even tipsy. I really wasn't a drinker. Every once in a while I would really indulge but for the most part I tried to keep myself away from things that were not good for my body.

*Ding ding ding.* Looking down in my dash I noticed my gas light on. I was so lazy I hated getting gas I would ride until I was reminded. As I stood at the pump the streets were dark and dim. I had this feeling in my gut that something wasn't right just didn't know what it was. I immediately felt like I needed to get home to my children.

Dominique had promised me that she would not have anyone in the house and she could watch her siblings. I still didn't trust her after I found that little thug in her bedroom both of them half naked. I went ballistic slapping both their asses the hell up. I tried to slap them to sleep. I had him running up out of my house in his boxers and cut up his damn clothes. The Iphone he left on her dresser got smashed on the concrete in my driveway. Her ass was screaming and hollering please don't hit her she was pregnant.

I stopped in mid swing and stared my daughter up and down. I honestly thought my ears were playing tricks on me. I knew that was not what I'd just heard come out of her mouth. She hadn't learned from me that having children was hard? She hadn't realized that when you're young you're really not ready to take on that kind of responsibility. Didn't she see how much I had endured by having her when I was 14 myself? Maybe she thought she was smarter than me what happened to me wasn't going to happen to her because she had it all figured out. Didn't she know that, that little boy could and would walk out on her whenever he wanted to?

Of all the things I had been going through that by far hurt me the worst. I expressed to my daughter my concerns but she cried and screamed how much he loved her and they were going to be a family. The disappointment and hurt that I felt I can't even explain it. All I could do was shake my head and walk away. She'd kept being pregnant from me for six weeks. I'd never let her get an abortion but I'd thought I was close enough with my children that they would feel comfortable coming to me about anything. I didn't talk to my daughter or even look her way for an entire week.

The communication barrier broke when she mustered up enough nerve to come into my room and have a heart to heart talk with me. It didn't stop me from being disappointed. It didn't stop me from hurting not just because she'd kept the secret from me but for her. I told Dominique that she would never have to worry about her baby and that she was to finish high school and go to college none of her dreams had to come to an end. I would help her with everything as long as there was breath in my body they would be alright.

It wasn't the end of the world and what happened was already prewritten by God because the devil could do nothing without His permission. I was her mother and I would see to it that every dream she ever had would come to pass. I had been through the same thing so what better person to be her mother than I? Whoever said history repeats itself wasn't lying but the outcome wouldn't be the same as mine.

I had done pretty well for myself but I had put up with a lot of nonsense. My daughter was smarter than me. She had much bigger dreams than me and she had a wonderful mother standing next to her that would cheer her on every step of the way even as she made mistakes. That was how we learned that was how we evolved as a people and she would be an inspiration to others just like I had been to her. They would hear her story and know that it wasn't over. She'd know that life went on and you didn't have to be a victim of your circumstances.

I just prayed that little boy didn't get in her head making her think he was the Messiah and have my baby's mind all twisted like Rodney had mine. I'd moved out of my mother's house got on assistance and got my ass beat every day even during my pregnancy. It started with a push, a slap, maybe a choke but before long the fist would come and I'd be walking into school with black eyes, busted lips, and bruises all over my body. That was no life to live for anyone. Especially a fifteen year old girl with a baby.

I finished pumping my gas and started on my way home. When I pulled up to the house it was dark my children must have been asleep. As I walked up to the door I couldn't shake the feeling that I was being watched. I turned around to see a man sitting in a car across the street looking directly at me. I didn't know who it was so I put a little pep in my step as I high tailed it to the front door fumbling with my keys to get in.

I didn't have my gun with me. Shit! I left it in the car. So much for that. *What good was it to have a pistol if I couldn't get to it in a time of need?* I thought. I looked back and he was still sitting in the car staring at me. He was dark skinned with a thin mustache and a big meat head looked like some kind of football player or something.

Antoinette must have heard me at the door because next thing I knew the front door flew open causing me to jump and scream. I pushed her back and rushed inside locking the door and turning the deadbolt. I ran to window and peered outside just as he was pulling off. My daughter looked at me groggily as I calmly told her to go get in the bed still peering out the window. No need to get the kids all worked up. Maybe it was nothing but you could never be too sure with people these days.

I lay on the couch with the machete I had underneath one of the cushions. If anyone decided to come in they'd be going out on a stretcher. All questions could be answered later.

## CAMERON

## (7)

It had been a busy night at the hospital we were working nonstop. I thoroughly enjoyed nights like that it made the time go by quickly. Once the day was over I began my short vacation of two weeks doing absolutely nothing but sitting around enjoying some much needed rest and spending time with my daughter.

I hadn't spoken with Marteen in a while and that was fine with me. She had dropped Yasmine off with her parents and hadn't returned for the past week. They said she'd called a few times but didn't give them a time frame as to when she'd be back. That was my opportunity to spend time with my daughter without being harassed by her silly mother. That woman could bring out the best and the worst in people. The more she stayed away the more peaceful my life. I welcomed the thought of her disappearing for a while. Although I really wasn't feeling the fact she just dumped our daughter off on her parents.

I was grateful for them. They seemed to be the sane pair of the trio. Although they'd do anything for their daughter they knew she was being irrational when it came to me seeing her and they would go behind Marteen's back so Yasmine and I could spend father daughter time together. They always acted as if they feared her coaching our daughter into keeping this big secret from her mother.

As much as it irritated me I let it go because I didn't want to ruin my chances of being with my child. My patience with my soon to be ex wife was wearing thin and she was pushing me to limits I never liked to go. Her lawyer had found every loop hole she could to keep these proceedings going and we hadn't even come up with a temporary custody agreement. The plan was for me to get custody. Personally I didn't think Marteen was fit to raise a child. She was immature, selfish, and void of emotion. My daughter didn't need to grow up in a home like that. Not when she had a father who loved her more than anything on the earth.

I couldn't understand why it was so hard for a father to get custody of his children. Couldn't these people see this woman was unstable? Sure she was a beautiful woman who represented class and sophistication but her character was questionable. What? Because she wore $1200 shoes and used proper grammar when she spoke she was more fit than I to be a parent? Let alone a loving and caring parent? The woman wouldn't even get a job for Christ's sake!

When my daughter told me she left her in the car and it was hot and she couldn't breathe I wanted to go break Marteen's neck. I called her she wouldn't answer the phone I didn't leave any messages that woman was slick she wasn't about to get me caught up. Not to mention I wasn't even supposed to have her so it was best that she hadn't picked her up. I guess she was thinking she had the upper hand and I'd let her to continue to think so until I came up with a plan.

I didn't know the particulars of the situation and I knew how children could sometimes stretch the truth. When my daughter told me that story I could still see the fear in her eyes. I wanted to know where they were and how long she had been in there but she had no sense of time or direction she was only three years old. I was supposed to be able to protect her from all harm. How could I do that when the law was on the side of a mad woman? I prayed that the woman I had married wasn't that foolish and it was all just a child with an overactive imagination. My heart told me my daughter was being neglected.

It's funny how when you remove yourself from a situation you start to see things and people for who they really are. I didn't like my wife at all. She was almost demonic in a sense. The way she played with peoples' lives. She had no regard for living she was reckless in all her endeavors. That was scary. She was a narcissist everyone was expendable.

I was excited to be sitting across the table at the little frozen yogurt shop watching my daughter devour her dessert. Our plans were ice cream and a matinee then do a little shopping. I always treated my baby girl like a princess. I heard the bell ring signaling someone had walked through the door. I looked up to see one of the most beautiful women I'd ever laid eyes on inside and out, Ava. She hadn't noticed me yet. I watched her holding hands with her son smiling and conversing about the difference between frozen yogurt and ice cream. It was cute I could see the love in her eyes even as he continually asked why. She didn't get frustrated she didn't ignore him she humored herself every time she answered him.

It was as if they were the only two people in the world that mattered. She hadn't even acknowledged the cashier not that she was trying to be rude but she wanted to make sure that her son had her undivided attention. I admired that in her even at work with difficult patients she was always so attentive. They might come in spitting venom but by the time Ava was done with them they'd be thanking her and giving her praises as if she was their very own guardian angel. She just had something about her that drew people to her.

I watched as they ordered their frozen dessert and took a seat near the window pointing at the cars riding by. "Oooh, that's my car," her son screamed excitedly pointing to a red shiny sports car. His mother pinched his cheeks and told him how it was her car because he cheated since he knew she wasn't paying attention. I couldn't help but want to join them. Didn't know how to approach her but since I had my daughter and she had her son I was sure I could come up with some type of slick way to get her to agree to a date even with the two little ones without biting my head off, giving me the cold shoulder, or making up an excuse.

She couldn't say no if I sent Yasmine to their table to see if they wanted extra company. There were two more empty seats. I whispered in my daughters ear and sent her over to the table as I ear hustled from the corner.

"My daddy said can we sit at your table?" she said in the sweetest voice ever. Not quite how I wanted it to go down she wasn't supposed to say *my daddy said* oh well from the look on Ava's face it was apparent she was going to say yes.

Looking in my direction as my daughter pointed me out Ava pursed her lips together and squinted her eyes shaking her head. She whispered something into Yasmine's ear and sent her back to our table.

"Daddy, she said come ask her yourself!" she said cupping her hands over her mouth and giggling. I guess she thought it was funny to see her daddy getting played. My daughter had the greatest sense of humor. When we were together even though she was three we always had a good laugh. It was like being a child all over again.

Standing up I slipped my hands up under my daughter and carried her over to Ava and her son. "Hello, Ms. Ava," I said looking her in her eyes and giving her big smile. "My daughter and I wanted to know if you all wanted some company." I said making eye contact with her and then her son.

"No I didn't daddy!" Yasmine said. "You said to ask her," she said busting me out.

It was something I knew Ava was already aware of but it was cool. She knew I had been trying to get her attention for a while now. Ava burst out in laughter while her son sat there looking at me like I was the enemy. I had heard about little boys being protective of their mothers but damn. I think little man wanted to square up with me.

"Well?" Ava asked clearly amused by what was taking place.

"Do you want some company?" I asked sliding into the seat next to her son.

Little man responded no while she gave me a yes. Ava looked at her son as if to say it is okay. She went on to explain to him that we worked together and how I was the "nice" doctor she sometimes talked about. So she did think about me too. That was a start. Her son still wasn't buying it. I had rained on his parade but I was determined to win him over as well as his mom.

We sat there laughing and talking for hours it seemed like. Eventually who I'd come to know as Jaquan lightened up and was looking as if he was thoroughly enjoying himself. He was seven years old but most definitely very mature for his age. I found out he got good grades in school and hadn't missed a day all year. He sat there giving me his highlights while poking his little bird chest out. I also found out Ava had two other children, daughters one which was pregnant.

When he let that cat out the bag Ava shot him a look that even scared me. I laughed on the inside I remember running my mouth too much in grown folks business and moms giving me that look. I wondered how old her daughter was I knew Ava was only 28 or 29 years old. I saw it all the time though things happened. That could've been why she was so uptight lately. Either way it hadn't changed my perception of her. I still put her on pedestal although I didn't really know her outside of our professional relationship. That was going to change since I had been at the right place at the right time.

We ended up spending the rest of the afternoon together going to the movies and to the mall as planned. We even hit up Toys R Us and let the kids fill up a basket like it was Christmas in the summertime. They were worn out but for Ava and me it was as if we had just gotten started. I knew it wasn't just me feeling like our night should continue to go on. As I drove Ava and Jaquan back to her car I mustered up enough nerve to ask her out on a second date without the children.

"Cameron, I really had a great time," she started wincing as she continued on. When I stopped at the light she turned to look me directly in the eyes. "I'm not ready to date anyone right now." She added.

That was not what I wanted to hear and I didn't want to pressure her so I chose my words very carefully as I proceeded through the light keeping my eyes on the road I nodded. "I understand that," I said but I couldn't take no for an answer my brother Kymani would call me weak he always said I was a sucka for a pretty lady. "Ava, I am not asking you to do anything you don't want to do just dinner." I responded.

I could tell she was weighing her options. At least I'd gotten that far. This woman just didn't know how long I had wanted to show her a good time. I truly felt like she deserved some peace in her life. Although she would never confess and she'd always put her game face on around others. I'd learned a long time ago the eyes never lied and she was in turmoil more times than not. I watched her sacrifice her happiness for the benefit of others.

She didn't answer she sat in the passenger seat contemplating my proposition which was fine with me at least it wasn't a flat out no like I'd usually been getting. "No pressure," I started. "If you don't have fun I will never ask to take you out again." I said placing my hand on her knee. She looked down at my hand and I quickly removed it. I wasn't trying to be fresh just reassuring.

"Mr. Powers," she said with a blank expression on her face. I knew what was coming next. If she didn't say yes this time I wasn't about to keep begging her. I mean I had been the perfect gentleman I thought we were having a great time. I didn't want to run game on her or try to hurt her in any way. "I'd love to go on another date with you." She said breaking into a big smile.

I kept my composure I was jumping up and down on the inside but on the outside I just nodded and smiled as I wrapped my hand around hers as we drove. I was kind of expecting her to pull away but this time she didn't. Her hands were small. I rubbed the inside of her soft palm and I heard her let out a small moan. Yeah I knew she was feeling me. For a second I imagined myself deep inside of her making her moan nonstop.

*Damn nigga get your head out the gutter.* That's what I was telling myself but that woman was doing something to me. Why else would I have been working so hard to get a chance with her? She was entering my life at the right time. People may have thought I was moving too fast but I knew what I was doing. She wasn't a rebound because I wasn't pressed about my wife.

"Can I ask you a question?" Ava said interrupting my thoughts. I nodded in agreement. "What is your wife going to think about these little dates we're going on?" she said pulling her hand away from mine. Maybe for a brief moment she had forgotten I was married but the situation I'm not calling it a marriage anymore was dead.

I didn't bat an eye I didn't stutter not one time when I told her the story of Marteen and I. She sat there taking it all in as we sat in the parking lot next to her car. I liked the way she listened and empathized with what was going on in my life. This was the first person I could sit down and talk to without feeling like I was being judged or that they were biased. She asked me questions that really made me think about the decision I had made and helped me to confirm any doubts I'd had about the woman I decided to marry right then and there. I appreciated her for that.

I asked her about her love life and when she told me her story I don't know why but I became angry. I felt like I should have been there to protect her and to show her how love was really supposed to be. I was amazed at how she still stood tall and held her head high. She possessed strength about her that some women never obtained. She was still thriving still going relentless in her effort to find peace and happiness in her life.

I told her she would be just fine and to just relax and let peace just be peace. She soaked in the statement nodding her head and repeating it with her lips but not actually saying it aloud. Before we knew it her cell phone was going off and her other two children were asking her where she was at. I laughed on the inside it was as if she was the child and they were her parents.

She turned to me, "You know how it is when you're pregnant," she said attempting to hide the sorrow in her eyes and voice. "My daughters starving and doesn't want to eat anything but a chicken Alfredo pizza." She said pretending to be amused.

I didn't want our day together to end so I offered to take her to this little spot a friend of mine owned who made the best pizza in town and we could all eat pizza. "Being that none of us have eaten dinner," I added trying to plead my case.

Looking at the time she hesitated. "I don't know Cam. It's getting pretty late." She said looking at the clock on the dashboard.

It was almost as if I was begging but hey go hard or go home. Alone! Thinking about her! Wanting to be around her! What the hell I'd press my luck. "Look Ava, we won't stay long we'll get the pizza, eat and I will head home."

She finally agreed. I was feeling myself I guess hard work does pay off. She jumped in her car and followed me while I kept the two little ones who had fallen asleep long ago in mine. On our way back from the pizza parlor I noticed a car with a husky man pull up next to Ava and roll down his window. He had no tint on his window and although it was dark the street lights were illuminating the inside of his car.

When she looked over at him he put his fingers up as if he was pulling a trigger. I jumped out of the car and quickly started to approach the other car. I know dumb move anything could have happened but that's what I did. He sped off almost hitting another car backing up trying to get away. I got a good look at him and I didn't forget faces. Our town wasn't so large somebody like me couldn't find out who the cat was. His old beat up sedan was one of a kind and he looked so familiar.

*What the hell was he harassing Ava for?* I thought to myself. I walked up to her car as others blared their horns cursing and going around us and asked if she was okay. She was a bit shook up but I noticed her hand on a nine millimeter handgun. I was impressed. "Do you know him?" I asked looking her directly in her eyes.

"No I don't know him," she said breathing heavily. "But he is the same mothafucka that was sitting outside of my house the other night staring at me. I think he's been following me." She said looking around.

"We'll go to the house feed the kids and try to figure this out," I said having every intention to make some telephone calls of my own. I needed to find out what was going on with my Mrs. Right. I didn't need any extra drama but I wasn't sure if I could let her deal with anymore bullshit on her own either. I started back to the car but turned around. Leaning forward into her window I said, "You all are not staying home by yourself tonight," that was a statement.

Some could say I overstepping my boundaries because I didn't ask but sometimes a man had to do such things. When it came to the safety of those he loved and cared about there wasn't anything a real man wouldn't do to protect them. I hadn't always been a square and for a little while although focused on making a better life for myself I had to be out there in the streets getting money. I knew how it went out there. I had even worked a couple jobs for Mr. LeBlanc which was truly why he respected me so much. He loved his daughter but he loved his money more so that's why I never worried about what would become of me when I left her crazy ass.

Ava nodded her head in agreement hands shaking as she grabbed the wheel. I asked her if she was okay. She said yes. I got back in my car driving in complete silence until we pulled up to her home in a nice quaint little neighborhood. We carried the two little ones into the house while her daughters got the pizza out of the car.

"Mom!!!!!" Dominique yelled which caused both of us to run out the door. "This man just stopped in front of the driveway staring at us!" she said pointing at the brake lights at the bottom of the street.

"Just get in the house girls," I said remaining calm as not to excite them. They hurried inside with the pizzas and we locked the door. I couldn't help but think is all this going to be worth it? *What the hell did I get myself into?*

# LAUREN

## (8)

I'd been working both jobs nonstop. My productivity at my day job was slipping because I spent long nights working the club and doing private parties. My name was booming in the streets. I was a hot commodity. Chocolate was what they called me. Yes I was sweet as the candy. My life even sweeter I had a show seven nights a week. I was tired as hell but I had a new friend called "money" that kept me going so I wasn't really complaining.

I sat at my vanity in the dressing room putting on eye shadow. I had mastered the art of designing my face. That night I'd be a peacock looking like a Las Vegas showgirl until I stripped down to nothing but my eyes and headdress would still reveal the essence of the fantasy I planned to provide that night. Shit was getting crazy at the club. Bitches were acting up bumping into me trying to start arguments and hating on me because I still had that thang sewed up.

That bitch Kat was still on my ass trying to take her customers back because she thought she was reigning queen but it wasn't quite working in her favor. She thought because she was light skinned with long naturally curly hair she could just boot all the black hoes out but she had another thing coming. The blacker the berry well ya'll know how the rest of the saying goes. She was mad because she was used to fucking up the game by turning tricks. Well it was a new trick turner in town and I could suck a mean dick, ride it, and squirt all over it and do a much better job at it than she could apparently.

Her time was up. I guess she didn't like anyone playing with her money so she decided to get me up out of there. It didn't work though. My homegirl Porsha peeped game and let me in on the bitches little secret. Her and her little crew thought they were going to put me outta commission but them hoes had another thing coming. Supposedly they were supposed to run up on me beat me real bad so I wouldn't be able to work.

I'd told ya'll before I was a lover not a fighter so I had one better for them hoes. I'd never been one to take an ass whoopin' and I couldn't call my girls this time so I opted to handle my business by myself. I solicited a bodyguard to guard this beautiful body of mine. He was with me at all times except when I was working the club and what I was paying him secured my position as top notch bitch in the industry. He even kept the pimps off my ass. He was a big burly nigga who never smiled not even when I handed him his three hundred dollars a night. Money well spent considering now I was making about a grand at the club and about another grand for two hours worth the work after the club.

It wasn't even two hours I knew how to work these tricks. They'd call for a show the clock started when I got to the establishment. I'd go to the bathroom to get ready about twenty minutes then I'd set up another ten to fifteen minutes so I only had to work for 30 minutes. If they didn't come in 30 then there was another $500 fee just like that. I had become a shark in the underworld. Fuck you pay me was my motto. I wasn't a hooker I was a business woman and if a man black, white, Asian, Hispanic, or any other nationality had that paper there was nothing I wouldn't do to get it.

I was always told never do anything for free. While these little hot ass bitches were out fucking Raheem, Tommy, and whoever else for free falling in love, getting pregnant, and fighting other hoes I was getting money from these mothafuckas. That's what I did I was something like Robin Hood. I used to be poor but not anymore. I was robbing the rich by providing them with an illusion. I didn't give a damn about these bastards. None of my main tricks outside the club even knew I was a stripper. I'd let them believe that I was truly interested in starting a relationship with them and after I gave them the best head and pussy of their lives I'd finesse them out of the money that was owed to me. My presence didn't come cheap.

The club was packed just like every other Saturday we had some big names coming to make it rain on yours truly. They didn't know they were coming to see me before they got there but once they were in they were all mine. Athletes were the biggest tricks and rappers portrayed themselves like they had it like that but I had no problem taking their scrilla either. It took a bad bitch like me to put them in their place. Before I even started stripping I had the game on lock every concert I went to I'd snag me a so called star. Only to have them blowing my phone up and me playing them to the left every time. Of course unless they were talking money.

Fuck niggas get money was the lifestyle I'd always lived. As I worked the club scoping the scene I met eyes with someone I'd just recently met. When our eyes connected he smiled. I rolled my eyes and continued strolling through the club. It was inevitable that I walk past him to get to VIP so I'd catch up with him later. MAYBE! I wasn't pressed to be next his cocky ass so I just kept doing what I did best work the crowd of thirsty ass men.

I looked back over to where he'd been sitting and he was gone. *Good* I thought didn't have to waste my time on meaningless conversation. I was headed to the VIP area where the big money was when I felt someone grab my arm. Turning around I gave Dollar the once over as if to say get your filthy paws off my arm. His grip eased up a little but he pulled me into him whispering in my ear.

"I take it you choosin' tonight?" he asked.

Choosin'? Choosin' what? To go home with him? To make him my man? To have him fucking up my money being all up on me like that? He had the game all twisted. I was at work and the only thing I was choosing was to make my money that night go home pull black thunder out of my drawer and put myself to sleep. I snatched my arm away rubbing away the sting from his grip. Who the hell did this nigga think he was grabbing on me like that in my house? He better be glad I was on a mission or else I'd have security come fuck his ass up.

I kept it moving heading towards VIP. I could hear his laugh over the music. He was a sadistic bastard the more run ins I had with him the more I disliked him. There was something about him that was sneaky and yet he was sexy I wanted to know more. I continued on with my night grinding, bouncing, sliding, and most of all collecting my dollars with that man on my mind. He had a certain something about him that intrigued me. At the end of the night against my better judgment as I headed back to the dressing room to wind down I found him sitting in the same area watching my every move.

I leaned into him whispering for him to wait for me after the club. I knew he had it because he had dropped a pretty penny on those shoes he bought me a month or so ago.

It wouldn't be time wasted not to mention I could get some from someone I was at least attracted to. He nodded as if he knew how the night would have played out. I walked away thinking arrogant ass nigga. That was a turn on though no one ever came at me like that. They were always in awe of my beauty and my intellect really got them. Courtesy of all the knowledge Chaz gave me in those letters he used to write from prison.

I went to the back and hurriedly started getting changed so I could leave with Dollar. Kat and two of her flunkies busted in the dressing room talking loud and acting ignorant as usual. I looked at them through my vanity mirror as I wiped the makeup off my face with a tissue. I listened to them talk shit as they stared at me taunting me. It was me against three I wasn't about to open my mouth and say a word. I picked up my bag and walked towards the door to exit.

Kat jumped in front of the door blocking my exit. "What happened to all that shit you was talkin' the otha night?" she asked rolling her neck and bucking her eyes. If this bitch didn't look stupid as hell. I wasn't about to answer her dumb ass question. I had somewhere I needed to be. I sighed and tried to walk past her. She jumped back in front of me pushing me back with a lot of force causing me stumble and drop my bag.

Damn I had told my bodyguard Tree to go home because I was leaving with Dollar. Looked like I was on my own unless somebody else came up in that dressing room but because I liked taking my time and being the last one out looked like I would be on my own. I could scream but although the party was pretty much over the music was still thumping nobody would hear me. I guess I had to take whatever was about to come my way.

I sighed trying to get past Kat only to have her do the same thing. "Look, bitch don't put your hands on me again!" I barked sounding more confident than I really was. Do ya'll know those bitches started laughing at me? They thought fucking with me was some kind of sick game. Yeah I had been talking plenty shit when Tree was around but they had been talking shit too. I didn't have time to be fighting. My looks were how I made my money.

In between laughter Kat looked over at the twins Sapphire and Ruby pointing in my face she said, "What the fuck you gon' do Chocolate?"

I wasn't sure what I was going to do but if I had to fight I guess I had to fight. I was scared of those bitches but I wouldn't let them know that. With fire in my eyes I stepped to Kat and next thing I knew she was on top of my head. I tried to fight back but she was strong slinging me all over that dressing room knocking shit over. All I could do was curl up in the fetal position and cover my face.

In the midst of all the commotion I heard a man's voice and then my punishment stopped. I peeked from behind my arms to see Dollar in the middle of the room and those three bullying bitches huddled together in one corner.

"Dollar, I-I-I didn't know she was one of your girls," Kat stammered. She had fear in her eyes. She was a tough ass bitch I had never seen her shook like that. What was she talking about one of his girls? I wasn't one of nobody's girls I was my own woman. What was he some kind of pimp or something? How in the hell did they know each other.

"Oh you didn't know?" Dollar asked pretending to be understanding of her ignorance. Just when the tension left from her he walked over to her and slapped the taste out of her mouth knocking her and Sapphire to the floor. "Bitch, don't you eva in life assume a mothafuckin' thang about Dollar you understand me?" he said raising his hand again as the trio coward in the corner. They all screamed yes in unison.

I slowly stood to my feet as Dollar motioned for me to stand over the bitches that had just tormented me.

"Hit these hoes," he said nonchalantly. I hesitated thinking how that bitch Kat was going to beat my ass when he was gone. He gave me a reassuring look and said, "You fear this weak ass bitch?" he asked as he kicked Kat in the stomach causing her to fold up and cough. I didn't say a word I just stared on in disbelief. That dude wasn't a joke. I never was one to believe in a man hitting a woman but those bitches deserved everything they were getting.

"Hit these bitches," he said again this time a little firmer. I gave Kat what must have been a weak ass hit to him right in the top of her head hurting my hand. I winced in pain as I rubbed my hand. "Oh no you can do much better than that," he said pulling out a pair of brass knuckles and handing them to me.

"Now hit these hoes," he said egging me on. I hit listening to them wail only to not be heard. Once I hit them I didn't stop I just continued to hit them over and over and over again. It felt good. All those years of being bullied, all the times bitches would call me black tell me how dark and ugly I was BAM! All those times my mother sat back and allowed her brother to molest me WHOP WHOP! All those years I hated myself came out with every lash I bestowed upon Kat, Ruby, and Sapphire.

I didn't stop hitting until Dollar gently pulled me away. Snapping out of the violent daze I watched as those bitches lay in a pool of their own blood. I couldn't tell if they were breathing or not. Lord knows I didn't want to kill anyone. Oh what had I gotten myself into? But as quickly as I regretted it Dollars voice came to me, so smooth and soothing. *No one is going to ever hurt you again. All the hurt all the pain it's okay it's gone now. Dollar will make sure no one ever makes you feel unwanted or unloved ever again.* Was he saying these things to me or was my mind playing tricks on me.

When I finally came completely back to my senses he was wiping the blood from my hands and escorting me out the club through the backdoor exit. I got in my car and did as I was instructed and headed to the address that he provided me. Looking in my rearview mirror I noticed Dollar going back in through the backdoor. I didn't know what he was doing but I sure as hell wasn't about to find out. I had to get the hell outta dodge I had killed three bitches I didn't want to go to jail.

There was something brewing inside me. I felt powerful, I felt loved for the very first time. Maybe Dollar was the one for me.

## AVA

## (9)

Cameron and I had been spending a lot of time together. Things were going great turns out he was a very sweet and attentive guy. Every need me or the kids had he catered to it. The days that he had Yasmine which wasn't too often now that his ex-wife was back in town I really felt like we were a complete family. We hadn't seen the man in the old rusted sedan in a while but I still felt like I was being watched. I didn't know what the hell was going on but I was praying it would all just go away.

Dominique's pregnancy was going just fine and turns out the fifteen year old little boy I thought was a thug was actually a pretty nice kid. I met his parents we talked about the situation at hand and agreed that we would help our children and make sure their dreams didn't slip away from them. It seemed like ever since Dominique had gotten pregnant her relationship with Antoinette had become stronger. She was excited about having a niece and believe it or not I was excited about becoming a grandma!

Although I told my daughter we were going to have to think of a really cute name for her to call me because grandma sounded too old. We came up with the name Gigi. It fit me. I looked like I could be someone's Gigi well not really but it beat grandma. I was too young for all that.

Perry hadn't been bothering me as much at work but who knew with that man he would come out the woodwork on some bullshit every now and then. I hadn't been feeling too well all day. It started early in the morning when I was cooking breakfast. The smell of the bacon caused me to become sick to stomach. I had to rush to the bathroom and threw up for several minutes. Antoinette had to finish cooking for me. I needed to lie down before I went to work.

As soon as the smell from the hospital hit me I instantly got sick again. Ms. Pam one of the older nurses in my unit walked up to me asking if I was okay. I assured her I was fine but she insisted that my face was green and maybe I should take the day off. I told her I could make it through the day. I didn't have a fever or any other symptoms just an upset stomach. As I was walking to check on a patient in room #9 I felt myself getting lightheaded. Next thing I know I was waking up in one of the beds with Cameron, Pam, and Perry standing over me.

I tried to sit up but became nauseous leaning over the side of the bed and throwing up again. I knew I wasn't going to be able to be at work for the rest of the day. I couldn't even stand up without becoming sick. Pam suggested before I go I get a pregnancy test and be tested for the flu. I shot Cameron a look. He stood there looking stupid which pissed me off. I didn't know why I had an attitude with him but that goofy ass look was a sure start. Perry stood there looking like the dickhead he was.

The thought of me being pregnant hadn't even crossed my mind. With so much going on I hadn't even taken into consideration that I could be pregnant. I knew that one time Cameron and I decided not to use protection would end in disaster. I didn't need any more children right now! Hell my daughter was having a child of her own! What did that look like me and my fourteen year old daughter standing side by side with big ass bellies going to the damn OBGYN together?

I immediately got a headache. Against my better judgment having everyone in my damn business I let them check me out before I left to go home. Cameron came back in the room alone with the results in his hand. He didn't look grim but he didn't look happy either. The best word I could use was…TORMENTED.

"Let me guess," I said with an attitude. "I'm pregnant." I stated already knowing the answer. I was too old to have a surprise pregnancy. This was not how to start off a relationship, friendship, or whatever it was that we had.

"It looks that way Ava," Cam responded sitting down on the bed next to me rubbing my thigh and giving me a look of sympathy.

"Look I don't need you looking at me like that," I spat. "I don't need your sympathy it's not the end of my world." I added knocking his hand off my thigh.

Deep in thought he responded, "Whatever you want to do I support your decision," he said.

What the hell did he mean by that? Was he fucking serious? Whatever I wanted to do I had his support? I guess he was insinuating maybe an abortion. Hell no! I'd never had one never would get one. That was not something I would do. I should have went home and taken my own pregnancy test, started looking for a new job, and cut off all communication with his ass.

What he just said to me didn't even require a response. I wasn't about to go through all the dramatics. It was what it was. I was pissed at myself and him for us being so damn irresponsible. If he would have just left me alone like I asked him to in the beginning neither one of us would have been in that situation. I slid off the hospital bed grabbing my things and walked out the door leaving him sitting there in his own thoughts.

As I proceeded down the corridor I could feel Dr. Mitchell burning a hole through my back. I prayed that he didn't say anything to me because today would be the day I lost my job and caught a case. He was still harassing me every chance he got, making little snide remarks and acting like a complete asshole. I had enough going on in my life. I didn't need his bullshit at work.

I got in my car and started to cry leaning my head against the steering wheel causing it to honk. That was the story of my life it was always something. I cranked up the car and headed home in silence no radio just me alone with my thoughts. My phone started ringing it was Cameron I hit ignore. Maybe I'd talk to him later maybe not but I had things I needed to do. One was get on my computer and look for another job. No more procrastinating it was time to move on.

Pulling up to the house I noticed a BMW sitting in my driveway. As I walked closer I saw there was a very beautiful woman sitting in the driver's seat on an iPad. Knocking on the window I stood there waiting for her to respond. I didn't know what to expect so I had my guards up. She turned to look at me with cold piercing gray eyes and smiled. She looked disturbingly familiar. As she rolled down her window I decided to just cut to the chase so I could get in the house and lie down.

"Can I help you," I asked with a lot of attitude. This bitch was parked all up in my driveway like she knew me or something.

"As a matter of fact you can," she replied with a smirk on her face. Her body language let me know that I shouldn't let my guard down. "Are you Ava Tanner?" she asked although I knew she already knew exactly who I was.

"Who wants to know?" I asked. I didn't just go around giving strange people I didn't know my name. Who knows what she was sitting in front of my house for. I didn't like the fact that she was invading my privacy and if she went about her business the wrong way I'd show her exactly how much.

Opening her car door and sliding out I could see a small protruding belly which put me a little more at ease. The woman was pregnant she couldn't have come over to my home with no bullshit. Then again who knew times had changed people had changed they'd do just about anything. Extending her hand towards me she introduced herself as Marteen Powers.

Okay now I knew why she looked so familiar I'd been spending a lot of time around her daughter. At that very moment I noticed Yasmine in the backseat as she yelled out my name excitedly. Her mother shot her look that told her if she didn't sit back and shut her mouth she'd do it for her. Any other day but today I could've handled dealing with this woman. Why was this woman sitting in my driveway? Why did she think we needed to become acquainted with one another?

Without extending my own hand towards her I took a step back and looked at her like she was crazy. "What can I help you with?" I asked in my no nonsense sista girl tone. I really wasn't feeling her whole demeanor not to mention I didn't take too kindly to anyone I was dealing with ex's showing up in my driveway either. This bitch was really about to catch an ass whoopin' fuckin' with me.

Sighing Marteen responded, "It was brought to my attention that you were spending a lot of time with my daughter and my husband," she said looking me directly in my eye. I nodded in agreement trying to figure out where she was going with her conversation. She said husband I thought they were getting a divorce. I had slept at his condo been around their daughter. Hell we had had sex with each other on numerous occasions and I was pregnant. Oh hell no I knew his wife wasn't pregnant by him also!

She proceeded, "Listen, Ava I'd really appreciate it if you stayed the hell away from my family!" she spat. "Cameron and I are expecting another child and we are working things out." She said to me.

I was never one to be left speechless but what could I say? She was standing there in front of me with their daughter in the car and small round belly telling me the married man I was sleeping with wasn't going anywhere. They were planning on expanding their family. So where in the hell did that leave me? Sitting around with a fat belly and a married baby daddy who would probably disappear.

"I'm glad you understand," Marteen said smiling and slipping back inside her car. "Oh yeah this was your first and last warning Ms. Tanner. Stay the hell away from my family." She said calmly as she slowly backed out of my driveway.

I wanted to be mad at her. I wanted to snatch her out of that car and drag her up and down the sidewalk but for what? I had been the stupid one. Cameron was her husband not mines. I was sold a dream. He used me to kill time while his wife was out of town. I wanted to call him and go off but that wouldn't change anything. I could feel my chest starting to heave up and down as tears welled up in my eyes.

Was there a reason why things like this always happened to me? All the long nights we had laying in each others' arms talking about life my life in particular, me telling this man all my business and he was playing me. It took all I had not to get back in my car head to that hospital and put my foot in somebody's ass! Hell I didn't work their anymore anyway! I was done with that place. I'd call in take my last two weeks vacation and not even give them a notice. Not even let any of my closer colleagues know that I was looking for a part time job. Play everybody and when it was time for me to go back they would be short staffed. I didn't give a damn. I had it all figured out.

My phone started ringing. **Cameron.** I sent his ass straight to voicemail. There wasn't shit we had to talk about. Our little love affair was over he could go be with his family I didn't want any parts of what they had going on. My cell whistled. *I'm on my way. Cameron.* Was this guy for real? To save myself the agony of having to deal with this man and his wife I texted back. ***Don't even bother I just spoke with your pregnant wife. Enjoy your life together I hope it all works out.*** Then I shut my phone off I was not about to entertain all of that nonsense.

I walked in the house dropping my bag on the kitchen counter bracing myself trying to hold back my tears. I didn't have any strength I felt like my life was spinning out of control. I didn't know how much more I could take. I called Ashley her phone went straight to voicemail. I left a message asking my little sister to call me back. Although we weren't as close as I'd liked for us to be we were working on our relationship and I was happy about that.

Ashley was my half sister. While my father was cheating on her mother with mine I was conceived. He never could take responsibility and left before I was even born. I despised his ass what a weak ass man he'd rather abandon his daughter than step up admit to his infidelity and take care of his own innocent child. I'd searched for him many years and finally located him in an effort to establish a relationship.

His wife wasn't having it though. Ashley's mother lost her mind asked me why did I need a father after twenty two years what was it that I wanted and what was I looking for? It really had nothing to do with her and although I am sure she was angry about the entire situation her husband was the only guilty party. My mother was manipulated by his slick talking ass and finessed right on out of her eighteen year old panties. Then he disappeared on us both.

I'm sure that was why I had stayed with Rodney for so long. I never wanted my children to feel the abandonment that I felt. Even after my mother remarried I never felt quite right. As great as her husband was I'd known he didn't love me like I was his own child. My own father didn't love me. It was funny how history repeated itself. Here I was pregnant at twenty nine with a married mans child. The twist in this fateful story was this man's wife was pregnant too. I lay back on my bed and chuckled thinking of all the events of the day. When it rained it poured like a mothafucka I thought letting out a deep sigh.

The ringtone on my phone began to play. "Hey little sis," I said into the receiver trying to sound as happy as possible.

After a brief conversation we opted to have a girl's night with a few of her friends just to unwind. She was having a little shindig at her house a handsome male masseuse was coming in to give massages, finger foods, drinks, etc. That actually had me a little excited. I loved when my sister threw parties like that. She'd thrown a Diva Party for Antoinette on her last birthday she had a mobile nail technician come to the house, a makeup artist, photographer, played music, had servers she did her thing. Everyone had a great time.

That was my little sister always wanting everyone to have a great time. Even when we first met each other her mother and our father had been standoffish towards me. She warmed right up stepped in and our relationship grew. I was so proud of Ashley she was a wonderful attorney, an amazing sister, and an outstanding Auntie. When I'd called and told her Dominique was pregnant she didn't judge my parenting skills she cried right along with me. She took her niece out for lunch and vowed to help as much as she could.

She had her life in order. Ash was grounded she worked hard and the fruits of her labor showed. She was beautiful and single with no children. She'd been dating a professional basketball player but not once did she choose to be someone's trophy wife she was more concerned with making a way for herself. She never settled. That's what I loved about her although she was my little sister I admired a lot about her.

## MARTEEN

### (10)

I walked into the barely furnished dingy apartment for the third time that week. The smell of sour clothing was overwhelming but I had to do what I had to do. Chester had proved to be a valuable asset to me. He did whatever I said with no questions asked. He was exactly what I needed in my life at the time someone who was willing to let me dominate him mentally and physically. I wasn't toying with his emotions he knew I was a married woman. He was perfectly aware that this could end at any time.

I looked at him sitting on the dirty sofa facing the bulky color television that sat on a rickety wooden end table. He turned to look at me but I instructed him to continue to look straight ahead and keep his hands on his knees. He knew what was coming next. I walked slowly towards him and centered myself directly in front of him. He tried to touch me. I swatted him with my paddle.

"Ouch!" he yelped putting his hand back down. He looked at me with wet eyes. I laughed leaning towards his face.

"Shut up!" I said twisting my spiked heel into the top of his foot. The more I twisted the more he grimaced but didn't say a word. He knew what would happen if he did. I loved tormenting him it was pleasurable for me.

I sat my paddle down and slapped him hard across the face. He let out a whimper. I caressed his cheek softly then WHAM! I slapped the shit out of him again this time causing saliva to fly out of his mouth.

"Get up!" I demanded poking him in the chest and taking a small step back. He stood as I ran my hands over his naked body stopping at his dick. It was stiff standing at attention. I spit inside my hand then grabbed his long hard dick and began to stroke him as I stared into his eyes.

He tilted his head back in pleasure causing me to squeeze and pull harder. I was becoming wetter by the second. I pushed him back on the couch straddling him allowing him to enter me as I exhaled. I began to pounce up and down. As he thrust upward I'd come down as hard as I could squeezing my walls gripping his meat causing both of us to moan in pleasure. I could hear him mumbling how much he loved me and he would do anything for me.

Damn right he'd better do anything for me because if he didn't I'd cut him off just like I had before. As long as he continued to be my lap dog and do as I said he and I would be just fine. I asked him did he love me enough to kill for me as I continued to bounce pressing my breast into his face. He looked at me with the most sincere eyes I'd ever seen and answered simply with a lustful yes. That was all I needed to hear. I tightened the grip my wetness had on his member sliding up and down until we came in unison. We sat there for a moment spent my legs trembling.

"Did you really mean what you just said?" I asked searching his eyes for any hesitation.

He nodded his head laid me on that nasty ass couch and placed my nipple into his mouth. His tongue felt so good. I moaned with pleasure as his tongue played a tune of its own on my breast slowly making its way down to my hot spot. Even in his dark smelly apartment I found myself lost in ecstasy as he licked and sucked on my kitty until I came so hard I couldn't lift myself up.

Chester walked back into my life at the right time. Over the past several months I'd convinced him to find this home wrecking bitch Ava. It wasn't hard to find out that she was one of the nurses working at my husband's hospital. She was out of her mind if she thought she was going to steal my husband from up under my nose. I never did give Chester the entire story didn't want him to become blinded and not be able to get the job done for me. I lied telling him she'd crossed me in some other way and he was down to defend my honor from that point forward.

He'd started following her even while he was on duty. He knew her every move. He even knew where her children went to school, when they got home, and what they ordered for takeout. Chester even took it a few steps further threatening her putting a little fear in her heart. I didn't ask him to do that he made that decision on his own. We were a great team. Too bad it would only last until my husband came back home.

I stood up and began to slip back into my clothes. Chester stared at me begging me with his eyes to stay. "Why are you leaving?" he asked.

"I have some errands I need to run," I lied. I wasn't running any errands I was going to see my husband. From the look on his mistress's face I was sure she wouldn't be talking to him any time soon. If she did it wouldn't be conducive to her health at all. I was literally going to have that bitch killed.

"I can go with you," he volunteered.

What was with this guy? I gave him awesome sex and now I couldn't get rid of his ass. Didn't he know that if I wanted him to come with me I would have asked him to come? He knew the routine I couldn't understand why he just couldn't keep his mouth shut. Be seen and not heard. He was always ruining the mood by saying something stupid. If I hadn't needed him at that time he would have been history.

Pretending to care I told him I had to go pick up my daughter and that my ex and I had just split up and I didn't want to bring her around another man so soon. He looked like he was upset and hurt. Oh well it was his fault for being so dumb. It was obvious that he was only good for one well make that two things. Papa had always told me people can only do to you what you allow them to. That made it his fault that he was sitting there stuck on stupid with his feelings hurt.

His ignorance was to my advantage. I was still confused as to why he hadn't said anything about my daughter and Cameron being with Ava. Either he was more air headed than I thought and hadn't put two and two together or he just didn't give a damn. Whatever the case may have been he needed to stay on team Marteen or he'd be having some hard times to come. I always had something in my back pocket.

I slipped on my shoes in silence and briskly walked towards the door. I was a woman on a mission. "Marteen," Chester called out to me. I allowed my hand to linger on the doorknob acknowledging I'd heard him and was listening. "I love you." He said. I cringed at the sound of those words. I didn't respond as I opened the door and slipped out making my way home to shower before I headed to the hospital. I couldn't go make up with my husband smelling like another man.

When I got to my husband's job I sat in the car making sure every strand of hair on my head was perfect, every eyelash was in place and that I was looking spectacular. When I walked in all eyes were on me. That was to be expected I was someone to take notice to. I ran into Pam a long time associate of mine as I maneuvered my way down the corridor.

"Well, look at who we have here," she said stretching her arms out to greet me with a hug. I never really was one to take a liking to people but Pam was someone that even I had to like. I smiled big this time genuinely and embraced the older woman tightly. "What brings you to this old place, pretty lady?" she asked holding my shoulders at arm's length admiring me.

"I just dropped by to see my husband," I said coyly.

Smiling and pointing she said, "Well I am going to let you go so you can catch up with him because it looks like he is walking out the door," she said shooing me along.

I turned to see Cameron walking out the doors of the hospital. I glanced at the old cheap clock hanging on the wall. I wondered where he was going he never left work and not that damn early. A lot of times he pulled double shifts because they were always short staffed.

I trotted hurriedly in my five inch heels out the double doors behind my husband. When I got outside I called out his name waving my hand to signal him to stop. He turned and stood in the middle of the parking lot waiting for me. I slowed my pace down a little and once I caught up to him I smiled and tried to give him a hug but he pushed away looking down at my little belly.

"Surprise!" I yelled smiling placing my hands on my hips and poking my belly out a little further.

The look on his face told me he wasn't happy. Cam had always wanted kids. Why did he look so angry? Getting angry myself I continued, "What you're mad because your wife is pregnant?" I said putting extra emphasis on the words wife and pregnant. I knew how much he wanted a big family.

"Marteen, I don't have time for this," he said sounding disinterested. What exactly was it that he didn't have time for? He'd better rethink the situation. He was mine he said I do we had a child together he was stuck with me until the end until death did us part.

Trying to keep my cool I closed my eyes counting to ten. "I don't have time to deal with one of your little temper tantrums either," he said interrupting my woosah moment. He was really starting to piss me off. He was supposed to be happy we were pregnant. Matter of fact what did he have to do that was so important he couldn't talk to me and discuss the future of our family?

The more I remained quiet the more my mind drove me crazy. I could feel my body getting hot from the inside out. I was about to burst at the seams I could feel my breathing become erratic. Here I was trying to be a good wife and he just wouldn't give me a chance. I was trying to make things right but he wouldn't let me. He was acting like I walked out on the marriage and hurt him.

I stood there staring at him my heart beating so hard I could hear it in my ears. Tears of anger welling up in my eyes. I blinked fast to keep them from falling. I hated crying it was a sign of weakness. As they flowed and I felt the overwhelming urge to knock him upside his head I noticed him soften some.

He walked towards me and put his arms around me and urged me not to cry.

I really put on a show at that point in time. I let those tears flow like a river sulking into his embrace. Yes, I was getting my husband back. In between sobs I told him we needed to go somewhere to sit down and talk it was long overdue. I confessed how much I missed him and how I was incomplete without him. That was kind of true the whole truth was I missed his money and my ego was shot because he was always supposed to want to be with me no matter what. I was Marteen LeBlanc the woman every man wanted on his arm.

We agreed to ride down to the same little café where Ashley and I had lunch the day I'd run into Chester. The day was turning out exactly as planned. Cameron would come back home and Ava would be completely out of our lives. I was glad he hadn't mentioned anything about me going to her house and confronting her. Maybe she hadn't said anything.

From the looks of her she shouldn't say anything either it was obvious who was the better woman. She was probably too busy being wrapped up with her thousands of kids and that fast ass little girl she had that was walking around pregnant. One thing was for sure she'd better have kept far away from my husband or she was going to have bigger problems than she could have ever imagined.

There was quite a crowd inside we had a short wait of about fifteen minutes. I loved the ambiance of the place and the food was great. It had been a while since Cameron and I had spent quality time together. I wasn't complaining though I was just happy he wasn't continuing to play hard to get. I knew he wanted me back in his life just as much as I needed him back in mine. He did keep me level headed for the most part.

"When did you find out you were pregnant?" He asked eyeing me.

I hated when he looked at me like that. He never could read me but just him doubting me didn't sit too well with me.

"It's been a while," I said nonchalantly. It didn't really matter when I found out I was pregnant. All that did matter was that he knew now and because of it he needed to bring his ass home.

"So do you know who the father is?" he asked. I could've jumped out of that chair and stabbed him with a butter knife. Really? My husband actually fixed his lips to ask me if I knew who the father of our child was. He was still staring at me like he knew some big secret.

"Yes, I know who the father is Cameron!" I shrieked causing a couple patrons to turn in our direction. I lowered my voice and leaned forward. "Why wouldn't I know who is fathering this child..... Our child?" I said placing my hand on my belly and rubbing as if to comfort my unborn child. Really I was rubbing my belly to keep myself from being sick.

"I don't know Marteen," he said fidgeting in his chair and scrunching up his face. "I just don't trust you anymore." He added now looking me in the eye.

He had no damn right not the trust me. I hadn't done a damn thing that he knew about to date since his brother. He was just going to hold that over my head forever? It wasn't going down like that. I had told him I was the victim. Kymani had always given me those looks even when Cam was sitting right there. I'd even told him a time or two I didn't like how he stared at me. He just laughed at me said he stares at every pretty woman he see's like that. It was like some kind of set up from the very beginning.

Attempting to flip the script I opted not to go hammer in the café and replied with, "I really expected more from you Cameron." I had masked my anger with a motherly scold on my face. He shrugged his shoulders as if what I expected didn't matter and continued to pick at his food. "I love you," I said to regain his attention.

"Marteen, I really cannot do this with you anymore," he said to me with sorrowful eyes. He had no reason to look so fucking pitiful I was the one being hurt. "Just sign the papers," he whined almost pleading with me to be out of his life. It was like I was starting to annoy him. I could remember a time when he loved being around me now it was like I had an infectious disease or something.

I wasn't going anywhere any time soon. I wasn't signing any damn papers not as long as I was breathing. Every fucking thing he presented to those damn courts I would object to. I wasn't walking out of this battle without a fight. I never lost I refused to lose and it wasn't over until I said it was over and it was just beginning.

"Cam, I don't want to do this anymore either," I responded. "We need to work out our marriage."

He looked at me in disbelief. Losing patience wasn't something he did on a regular basis but my relentlessness was causing him to become unglued. Oh well too bad he'd unglued me on several occasions fair exchange wasn't robbery. However, I called the shots and I'd wear him down until he made the right choice which was to be with his family.

"Marteen," he shot back. "I don't know how much more clearly you want me to be. I don't love you anymore and this marriage is not going to work." He said trying to keep his voice down.

He didn't mean any of that. If he did he wouldn't have hugged me the way he had in the parking lot and we wouldn't be sitting down having a nice lunch when he should have been at work. As he stood up and dropped a few bills on the table for our meal I jumped up with him ready to follow him to the ends of the earth if I had to.

"I'm not just going to let you walk out on me like this," I told him.

"That's too bad because that's exactly what I am doing," he said snatching his arm from me and leaving the restaurant. That hadn't ended how I planned but at least he was becoming more open in hearing me out. All I needed was a little more time to work on him and things would be back to normal.

## Ava

## (11)

I was sitting in a corner booth at the café when I noticed Cameron and his wife strolling in for lunch together. I couldn't believe my eyes after all the phone calls and text messages I hadn't responded to he was still dealing with his wife when he lied and said he wasn't it. I was so glad I hadn't picked up that phone the last time. I would've been kicking myself in the ass at about that time. Just when I was beginning to think that there was such a thing as a good man one had to come in my life and show me otherwise. Show me that I was better off single. I slide out of that restaurant without either one of them noticing me. I didn't need those problems.

My cell began to go off and without even noticing who was calling I answered.

"Hello," I spoke into the receiver.

"Ava, why haven't you been answering my calls?" Cameron spoke into the phone.

I rolled my eyes in the top of my head and took a long deep breath. "Listen," I started. "And listen really good Cameron. Whatever you and that crazy bitch of a wife have going on leave me out of the equation. I am not here to play games with no grown ass man and his wife!" I shot. "I've got three kids at home and one on the way. I am not about to partake in whatever little games you two have going on. I've prided myself in being a woman these days and I want to keep it that way. So you two enjoy your lunches and raise your fucking children and quit calling my damn phone!" I yelled pressing end.

I was 38 hot. He had stepped away from his wife to call and question me? Who the hell did he think he was? What kind of bullshit was he on? He for sure wasn't about to run circles around me and handle me whatever way he sought fit or until he decided he didn't want to get cheated on and misused by that gray eyed evil bitch. I was trying to keep my cool but they were testing me. Pushing me to the limit wasn't something that would turn out too nice.

I headed back home to clear my mind. I had quit my job and hadn't been looking. I could live off my savings and retirement money for a little while I'd just need to make sure I was budgeting my money correctly. Too much was going on I needed some time to myself. I'd been stressed to maximum capacity. When I pulled into my driveway Cam was standing next to his car waiting on me.

This guy was just as crazy as his damn wife. Without hesitation I parked my vehicle in the garage and met him outside. "Why the hell are you at my house?" I hollered. Yeah I hated the neighbors in my business but him and his wife weren't about to continue to stalk me. My emotions were all over the place and I couldn't be passive anymore.

"Ava," he said way too calm for my liking. I was standing there blood pressure high, heart about to thump out of my chest, head hurting , and some more shit and he was saying speaking to me like he didn't have a care in the world.

Before he could even continue I cut him off, "Ava what?"

"What?" I asked. "First off you're married, secondly your damn wife is pregnant and coming to my home harassing me, and third you're still dealing with her!" I barked pointing my finger in his face damn near touching his forehead.

He put both his hands up in the air in retreat. "Whoa," he said looking confused. "Marteen is pregnant but I don't know if that is my child and if it is Ava that was before I even started dealing with you." He said sincerely. "I am not dealing with her I don't even know where you came up with that." He lied. There it was I had two damn eyes and them mothafuckas were just at that damn place I was at alone while they were having lunch together.

"You a damn lie," I rebuttled folding my arms over my chest and squinting my eyes. "I just saw ya'll!" I exclaimed. Apparently I had to spell things out for him.

"You should believe half of what you see and none of what you heard," was his response.

"What is that supposed to mean?" I asked wanting to punch him in his pretty little face. What was I thinking he was not going to pull the same stunts as Rodney? I refused to go through all of that shit again. Hell no!

"It means that I haven't seen Marteen in months. Yes the last time I saw her we had sex it was before you Ava and it was a mistake. You can't hold that against me!" He said throwing his hands up in the air. "She showed up at the hospital today and she followed me to the café just so I could explain to her that she needed to stop bothering me it was over. I owed that much to her to look her in the eye and let her know I didn't want her."

It made sense. Sounded like the appropriate thing for him to say, I hoped he'd meant it and it was the truth. He wasn't the type of man that talked just to hear himself speak. I had no reason not to believe him. He hadn't had a chance to talk to me because I wouldn't answer his phone calls, I didn't answer the door when he came over and I hadn't been to work. I could tell it was killing him not to hear my voice. He confessed that in such a short time he'd grown to love me and my children. I fit well in his life and he loved having me in it.

With Marteen being pregnant as well things would be complicated but it didn't mean that things wouldn't work out. The fact was I wanted Cameron and didn't give a damn about that crazy bitch Marteen no matter how much she tried to spook me. It was evident she hadn't convinced him to be with her. She needed to let that shit go.

He stared into my eyes waiting for a response. I was unsure of myself standing there in turmoil. I couldn't bring myself to look him the eyes. I'd always been so strong but now I felt vulnerable like a child. I didn't want to feel that way. I wanted to be secure with what we had. I needed to know that whatever it was we were about to go through would be worth it because I couldn't to get hurt again.

"Ava," he started pushing my chin up with his finger so I could look him in the eyes. "I'm not here to hurt you I just want to love you." he said.

I snatched my head away from him opening my mouth to speak but was taken off guard by a silver BMW speeding towards us. Interrupted by the screeching of tires from the car my eyes darted behind him and I could feel them becoming small slits as I glared at the driver. Marteen was pulling into my yard halfway parked on the grass. She jumped out on a rampage her fair skin now bright red. I took a deep breath. This was woman was out of her mind. Maybe he'd fucked up by sleeping with her the last time but she needed to move the hell on. She was fully aware that he didn't want her and yet she was acting as if he had given her some reason to believe they would get back together. Did he? Men were known to say one thing but make a woman believe another.

"I warned you bitch," she yelled pointing her finger at me. Things were about to get potentially ugly this was the second time this crazy ass woman had showed up at my home on some bullshit. She didn't know me and I was beginning to stop looking at the situation like the woman I was and was considering bringing the beast out of me.

Before Cameron could even begin to diffuse the situation I swept around him and charged towards Marteen. I knew Marteen had a sharp tongue but could tell she had never been a fighter. Her entire demeanor spoke volumes. Sure she was an evil vindictive and vengeful little bitch but I knew she didn't have it to get with me when it came to throwing hands. I was a hood girl from the very beginning. Before I knew it I had Marteen's back against the hood of her crooked parked BMW ready to pound her out.

Cameron ran over to us before things could get any more physical. Marteens' arms were flailing through the air as he grabbed me by the waist lifting me up and turning me around receiving several hits to his back as Marteen tried to hit me. I remained calm she wasn't a threat to me. I didn't really care and had had enough. What she was experiencing was the calm before the storm. My breathing was heavy and my chest was heaving. He put me down assuming I really wasn't tripping and subdued Marteen.

His pregnant wife was going insane. He looked surprised like he'd never heard her speak like that let alone act like some mad woman. She reminded me of a woman who was always smooth about things even when her logic went AWOL like she maintained a certain dignity about herself. That was all gone today. It was amusing to say the least.

"Get your crazy ass wife," I taunted laughing with a smirk on my face pointing at Marteen and walking towards the house. He should've been thanking God he didn't have two of us to maintain because I'd drag her little high sadity ass up and down my sidewalk and then mop that mothafucka with her ass. "When you're done come in the house babe." I added looking over my shoulder taunting Marteen even more.

That sent her over the edge she screamed and pulled and hit him trying to get at me. "Let her go," I encouraged calmly from my doorway.

"Cameron!" she screamed. "Let me go! You are going to allow this home wrecking whore speak to me like that?" she asked with genuine hurt in her eyes. I couldn't understand why she was so damn hurt? How many times did he have to let her know that it was over before she got the picture? I mean he was at another woman's house.

"Marteen," he yelled snapping her out of her jealous rage.

Her body jerked as she stood in front of him with a blank expression covering her face. I'm sure he probably didn't want to hurt her but he'd better not have lied to her and tell her what she wanted to hear. She had not come to understand that things were dead between them. He told her he would always take care of his children and she wouldn't have to worry because as long as she had his kids she would be taken care of.

That was something that wasn't going to go down as long he was with me. She would have to get her high class ass a job and help take care of herself. The children I could understand but her well we'd talk about that soon enough. She seemed to have calmed down a little slapping his hands away from her. "So you just chose your whore over your own family," she whispered in between clenched teeth.

He sighed closing his eyes. As they reopened she slapped him causing his eyes to damn near pop out of out of his head. Before he could even react that crazy woman smacked him again. He let it go maybe he understood that he too had fucked up. He should have never had sex with her giving her hope. She was clearly delusional. He had contributed to her madness.

"Marteen, I'm sor-" he began to say and she slapped the hell out of him once more.

She told him to save his sorry for someone who wanted to hear it like the whore he was sleeping with. She turned to get in her car telling both of us we had chosen the wrong woman to fuck with. She pulled off slowly and disappeared down the street.

He turned to see me standing in the doorway. As he approached cautiously I opened the door wider so he could enter. He looked spent. That had taken a lot out of him. His nerves were wrecked.

"If she comes to my house again Cameron it is not going to be pretty," I said closing the door. He'd never seen me angry especially to the degree I'd been in my front yard not too long ago he told me he didn't want me to become unglued ever again. Marteen had pushed me to a limit neither one of them knew existed.

He shook his head letting out a deep breath. Life had become a little crazy for everyone as of lately. He was a well respected highly paid physician and had baby mama drama up the ying yang. Not the regular drama a man of his stature would have but the woman he said I do to was trying to fight people in the streets. I laughed on the inside because he was too weak to keep my dick in his pants. Typical I thought.

He should have had his affairs in order before he pursued me but a man wants what he wants when he wants it and I guess he couldn't let me get away. All I needed to know was that despite what was going on he wanted me in his life. He told me I gave him balance and made him happy. It had been a long time since he was happy and he wasn't about to let Marteen or anyone else come between that.

He apologized to me for all the drama that had just transpired. We sat and talked for about an hour about what had taken place even laughed a little about the situation.

"You almost seen that hood chick come up outta me," I said stifling a chuckle. "I wasn't raised in the suburbs." I added with a raise of my eyebrows and nod of my head.

"Where are the kids?" he asked changing the subject. I was glad too because Marteen was getting no more talk time in my house.

"They're at my mother's house," I answered giving him a sly smile.

He knew what time it was. I was thinking makeup sex. I could see him becoming stiff as he adjusted the hardness in his pants. I looked down licking my lips.

"Are you hungry?" I asked slowly walking to the kitchen. With each step my ass jiggled. I got so wet with him and he fit me like a glove. The way he'd make me moan when he was burying himself deep inside of me no one ever made me feel that way.

"Hell yea I'm hungry," he answered standing up to take the short stroll to the kitchen behind me. When he got to the kitchen he was pleasantly surprised. I stood there with no clothes on and a plate in my hand.

"You ready to eat?" I asked taking my index finger and sliding it over my clit and bringing it to my tongue. "Want some? It's really good!" I added staring him in his eyes.

I didn't really have to ask hell yea he wanted some. He had just gotten beat down in my front yard because he couldn't live without it. He didn't answer my question he rushed me picking me up and laying me on the island in the kitchen. He kissed my lips long and hard. Our tongues dancing and sliding over each other as we moaned making smacking sounds as we explored one another. He broke free pulled his shirt over his head exposing his bare chest.

Even the way this man looked at me turned me on. My eyes were low and I could feel myself biting my bottom lip as I rolled my hips slightly while he removed the rest of his clothing. I was ready my wet spot dripping juice anticipating him entering me. He was hard as a rock. I wanted to feel him. He pulled me to the edge of the island and parted my lips with his tongue.

My body quivered. "Mmmmm," was all I could say. He started off slowly. Licking then sucking me as I rotated holding the back of his head with one hand while I playing with my nipples with the other. "Cameron," I whispered with a shallow breath he pulled my hood back and began to suck on my clit as he inserted a finger gently stroking.

I was becoming wetter by the second my body was tensing up. I pulled his head in closer to me then tried to push it back. I was going to cum. He was eating me so good. He moaned telling me how good I tasted. My hips moved faster as he sucked harder.

"Caaammmm," I moaned. He didn't answer he continued to lick, suck, and finger my pussy. "Mmmm you're going to make me cum," I gasped trying to maintain my composure.

He told me to cum don't hold back as he continued to do his thing. My body stiffened and I stopped. My hands gripped the sides of the island as I released what had to have been years worth the pent up aggression. I squirted in his mouth. He didn't stop though he continued pleasuring me with his tongue.

I tried to get away but I didn't have anywhere to go. He slowed his pace and allowed me to revel in the moment as my body jerked with pleasure. He stood up and entered me with one long stroke. I gasped as he made love to me on that island in my kitchen for the next 45 minutes before we moved to the living, the shower and finally the bed.

# LAUREN

## (12)

I was still on my power trip soaking up the moment I had finally gotten the upper hand over someone. Dollar had showed me a side of me that I didn't know existed. I wasn't weak and I couldn't be victimized anymore. He provided me with the power to make people respect me. People hadn't started to feel me but they were a lot more cautious in how they approached me or responded to me. Even at work no one knew for sure but they assumed I'd had something to do with the three missing dancers. I'd never tell what was really going on they could continue to speculate.

Dollar and I had been spending a lot of time together. He came to my house, took me to nice places, and bought me beautiful and expensive gifts. I didn't treat him like I treated most men though. I had a profound respect for my knight in shining armor. I was like a little girl in love for the first time. Okay so maybe he was a tad rough around the edges not to mention a pimp but so damn what he was there for me when nobody else wasn't.

He even helped me make more money than I ever thought possible. I was still working at the club but had cut it down to three times a week. Dollar would make his presence known every single night to make sure no one bothered me. I didn't even need security anymore his presence was good enough to keep everybody off my back. He booked me for elite private parties and held on to all my money so I wouldn't blow it. He was the perfect man.

Things had been going great. I was feeling better than ever. My man had bought me Christian Louboutin's I believe the average chick calls them red bottoms because they can't pronounce it let alone afford them. I was wearing Stella McCartney dresses; carrying $3000 Nancy Gonzalez crocodile tote bags. My game was up to a new level. I was beyond that bitch I was living like a superstar. Even the bitches at the club took notice to the new me. I was confident before but now I was a goddess.

I had quit my day job I didn't need that bullshit. I had come in late one day and my boss had the nerve to call me into her office questioning me about me wanting to keep my job. Told me that my productivity had been down and if I wanted to continue to work for the company I needed to get it together. Was that bitch out of her mind. Get what together?

I asked that bitch if it looked like I needed that job. I wasn't trying to be walking around like her broke ass, shoes leaning to the side with that stiff ass hair sitting on top of her head looking like a hat. She had me 100% fucked up. I knew she was jealous but damn. She didn't have any name brand shit she was just there. Hating on me because she wasn't that bitch. Sounded like a personal problem to me.

She told me I could get my things and get out of her office. That bitch busted her ass for that simple ass paycheck day in and day out. She didn't have anything to show for it but a pile of bills. I was getting money she could never get working there. I told her if she wanted to become a real boss bitch to give me a holler, flicked my card in her face and walked my chocolate pretty ass right the hell up out of there.

Unlike that ignorant broad I didn't need to bust my ass everyday to get by. I had a man who made sure I was more than taken care of. I got to wear the best of everything. I got to sleep up in the most beautiful hotels, eat at the finest restaurants, and meet important people. No one knew her. Old fat ass bitch. She was just jealous like everybody else. Even Dollars little hookers were jealous.

It wasn't my fault that they didn't have what it took to make him happy. If they kept themselves up they wouldn't be out on the stroll scuffing up the pavement looking to turn twenty dollar tricks. If they tried to be more like me they'd get to have the best of the best. If they knew how to keep their mouths shut they wouldn't get beat. Play their cards right and life would be grand.

Why would I believe they could even do such a thing? All bullshit aside those bitches weren't built like me. They could never be me. Their lives revolved around getting their next hit. They were strung out looking nasty oily skin, teeth nasty, hair stringy and a mess. Not all of them but his oldest working girls. Somewhere along the lines they fell off. They complained under their breaths but they should have been happy he still allowed them to work for him. A man of his caliber didn't need those bitches they needed him. He took care of them as a matter of fact he took care of all of us in his own way.

It was early in the day and I had a long night ahead of me. A client had booked me for four hours. The date would long but well worth it I hoped he wasn't a weird sadistic ass bastard. Usually my clients who spent the most money were just that. Strange as hell. They made me feel uncomfortable but the fact of the matter was money talked and I was willing to do any and everything it took to get that paper. Who better to give their money to than me?

Dollar was always telling me how beautiful I was. He said I made the most money out of all of the girls. As long as I kept our clients happy there would be more to come. We could change the world one client at a time. Make millions of dollars together getting these tricks to come out of their pockets and I could pay for my daddy to get well. He was a wise man knowing a little about everything. There wasn't a place we could go that he wasn't able to talk someone into giving us their money. He made them believe they needed me because secretly they did they just hadn't known it yet.

It had been a while since I'd seen my parents but I'd call them every once in a while. Daddy's health was still pretty bad mama said it was getting worse but she always over exaggerated everything. I'd go see pretty soon for myself. I had just been so busy making this money I didn't have time to go see them. Plus Dollar told me that I needed to stay on top of my game in order to keep the clients happy so we could keep stacking paper. It was the only way to accomplish what I needed to do.

I was sitting in my vanity putting on my makeup when Dollar walked into the room. He was a handsome man. I admired him from the mirror. He had made my life so much better. I put my powder down and smiled at him as he rummaged through a suitcase that sat on the bed. I asked him how his day was going but he completely ignored me. I knew better than to keep talking to him when he was in one of his moods. I'd seen girls get their teeth knocked out if they spoke when it wasn't the time to speak.

I never got that though. One day I asked him why you would do such a thing you don't want to give our clients ugly toothless hoes. He told me it was fine they could always get false teeth when they took them out the head would be better. Sounded rather ignorant to me but I guess it made sense. Nobody wanted their dick scratched up.

My phone started ringing it was my mother. I answered the call whispering into the receiver as not to aggravate Dollar. As good as he was to me I saw what he was capable of doing. I didn't want to be in the position that some those broads found themselves in. Mama told me daddy's condition had taken a turn for the worst. It sent my heart sinking down into the pit of my stomach. Exactly what did that mean?

I hated when mama spoke in riddles instead of coming right out and telling me what the hell was going on. I didn't have time for this today. Totally going left in the conversation she started asking me where I was working because she called my job and was told that I was no longer with them. I completely avoided the answer to that question and asked about my father.

Instead of answering me she told me I just needed to get over there so we could talk face to face. I didn't like being left in the dark like that. I told her I was on my way and hung up the phone before she could ask any more questions. I stood up to finish getting dressed. I needed to slip on something to head over to mama and daddy's when I noticed Dollar staring at me. Normally I wouldn't think twice about him staring at me I was most definitely something to stare at but I noticed that menacing look in his eyes.

I'd seen that look before when he was ready to make an example out of some of the other girls. I walked towards him cautiously pretending that I wasn't looking into the eyes of the madman I'd seen emerge from him in the past. I wrapped my arms around him placing my head inside his chest so I didn't have to look him in the eyes. Holding back tears as I spoke.

"Daddy, I've got to head over to my parents house," I said inhaling deeply as I rubbed my face into his chest. "Mama says my father is really sick, I need to find out what's going on." I said.

Before I knew it Dollar had a hand full on my hair wrapped in his fist. He had this look on his face. I couldn't really explain it I had seen him look at the other girls like that but never at me. I thought I was special at least that is what he told me. He would never do me like he did them.

"So, what do you think this is?" he said through clenched teeth as he pulled my hair so hard my neck twisted into an awkward position. I placed my hand over his trying to pry myself loose but his grip just got tighter.

"Dollar!" I grimaced as I tried to free myself. "My father is sick!"

He wasn't trying to hear none of that. He told me he didn't give a fuck about my daddy being sick. I had to go make his money. Yes he said his money! I was doing all the work and he was getting paid off the fruits of my labor. I worked hard and I never asked for a day off even when he had me booked every fucking day of the week and I couldn't even go check on my sick father?

Yeah he had taken me to the next level but he hadn't taken me any further than I could have taken myself. He had me bent if he thought I wasn't going to see my parents. I wasn't about to fight him because I knew that I'd be defeated before the fight even got started. I knew just how to play my cards. Go along with the flow and dip. He didn't have to worry about seeing my tight little black ass anymore. Our little arrangement was over.

As he barked orders at me and explained why he hadn't knocked my teeth down my throat my mind ran a mile a minute. I had to get out of the situation and fast. It was all good when he was flexing on those other bitches but not me. I wasn't built for this kind of shit. I was the ugly duckling who turned into a beautiful swan and I was used to people bowing at my feet in the present. What was going on with between Dollar and I was something I wasn't accustomed to in that day and age and definitely wasn't something I was going to allow myself to endure.

"Daddy, I'm sorry," I shrieked allowing him to fold me up on the bed.

"Dollar knows you sorry bitch!" he said spitting on me. "Where's the rest of my fucking money?" he said getting closer than I liked.

I didn't know what the hell he was talking about. I didn't touch any money but if I had it wouldn't have made a difference any damn way because technically it was my money I was the one busting my ass getting facials and shit for it. I tried to tell him that I didn't know what he was talking about but he delivered a blow to my head that caused me to see stars and little blue birds chirping in mid air around my dome.

I curled up into a ball on the bed to protect myself. I waited for more blows to come but none came. I peeked from behind my arms to be greeted by a vicious fist to my face causing blood to squirt from my mouth and nose. What the fuck had I gotten myself into with this fucking nut? I guess the ass whooping was in full effect at this point. I thought I could play my cards right and be spared but I guess I was the right bitch at the right time that needed an ass whooping.

Keima Campbell

If Dollar had taught me anything it was that I could fight back and I actually wasn't too bad at doing it. That is when I sprang into action landing some blows of my own. None of which compared to his but hell at least I was trying. My hits seemed to fuel his fire because his hits were becoming more damaging. I could only imagine what I looked like at that point. But I didn't stop swinging he was going to have to knock me out.

I was being slung from one end of the room to the next. Punched, slapped, and kicked over and over. For every one good hit I got in I took four or five. Finally I gave up the fight and just lay there taking in the last couple blows. It was apparent that he was tired too. I think I was a little more to handle than he had anticipated.

"Choc," he said in his deep raspy voice. All of a sudden he didn't seem so sexy and intriguing any more. "Get your ass up and clean up this mess. Then I need to you ready for your date tonight." He added tossing a towel in my direction.

Was this monster out of his fucking mind? Get ready for what? I wasn't going anywhere for him, with him, or with anyone else for that matter I was going the fuck home! He could scare all of those other bitches into staying but he wasn't about to scare me into being with him one more night. Silly of me to have thought that I was the exception.

"Oh and don't even think about leaving," he added. "You know I'm fully aware of what went down between you, Kat and her jewels." He laughed.

This grimy mothafucka had set me up. "What you trying to blackmail me?" I said with more attitude than he expected. "If I go down so the fuck do you!" I added sounding a lot more confident than I felt.

"You don't want to try Dollar," he said laughing off my statements. "You can if you want ain't no telling what might happen though," he taunted sliding his index finger down the side of my face.

I flinched at his very touch but not because of the pain or because I was afraid of him but because eerily enough I hadn't been afraid not one time during our altercation. I just wanted to avoid what I then knew was inevitable. I looked at him with fire in my eyes trying to control my breathing.

The trouble with a pimp he always thought he had the upper hand. Thought he was stronger thought he was wiser when reality he was only what his hoes had made him out to be. If he didn't have a bitch hanging on to his every word if he didn't have a bitch who believed that he was that nigga then he wasn't shit. Those other bitches may have believed that he was doing them a favor but I didn't. When it came to my daddy I didn't have any understanding whatsoever.

My daddy had killed my mother's brother and did prison time for it because he molested me. I had a daddy I didn't have men issues I had mommy issues. My father's sins were probably why my mother and I weren't so close because she thought it was my fault her brother was dead. She said that was her blood and I had caused the family far too much grief. However, she still loved my father I never could understand that. She never let my father know her true feelings. But as for me. She'd let my black ass know every chance she got.

Dollar wasn't keeping me from my daddy. I'd be one dead hoe before I let that happen. I was leaving that house in the next couple of hours rather he liked it or not. My cell phone was still sitting on the vanity. I did as I was told and started cleaning up the mess. He watched me like a hawk every move I made he watched wearing this disgusting look on his face. If I didn't know any better I'd think he was smiling at me.

He was a sick ass bastard. At that very moment I hated him that knight in shining armor turned into a dragon that needed to be slain.

# LAUREN

## (13)

My big break came when Dollar left the house to go handle business. I had put some ice on my face and surprisingly I didn't swell up too bad. I had a couple bruises here and there and my lip was busted but it wasn't anything I couldn't mask with a little bit of makeup. I made myself up real pretty so he'd believe I was getting ready for the date I had set up for later that evening.

He never even thought to take my cell phone. When I heard his car pull out the driveway I ran to the window to make sure he was gone. I dashed over to the vanity and started dialing Brooke's number. The phone kept ringing as I prayed for her to answer. That shit kept going to voicemail. I hung up and dialed the number again she still wouldn't pick up!

I didn't want to make the next phone call but I didn't have a choice. I called Ava. She would ask a million damn questions and have to lecture me about the decisions I made and how they affect everyone around me rather I wanted to believe it or not blah blah blah. At the time I was desperate and if she could come swoop me up then I for damn sure was down to call her to come get me the hell up outta there.

"Ava!" I yelled into the receiver.

"Damn" she said. "Why are you screaming in my ear?"

"Listen I need you to come get me now it's an emergency," I yelled peeking through the window.

She kept asking questions that I didn't feel like answering at the moment. I told her the address and hung up in her face I packed up as much of my shit as I could ready to scat my ass right on up out the front door. I would peek out of the window every few minutes just to make sure he wasn't pulling back up.

He never had a problem leaving me alone before and obviously he didn't believe he'd had a problem at that time either. Sure we'd had our first and last disagreement but I gave him no reason to believe I would buck. As I was packing I saw someone standing in the doorway out the corner of my eye. Damn I forgot Maria was still in the house. I still continued to rummage through the room throwing everything I could into the bag. She stood in the doorway staring at me with a smirk on her face.

I never could stand that Puerto Rican bitch. She thought she was better than me always having something slick to say. Swinging on Dollar's nuts like a little monkey. Telling on everybody when they were doing something she thought Dollar wouldn't approve of. It still didn't get her too much farther than I and I didn't put in half as much work as she did. I continued to get my shit like she wasn't there. I didn't give a damn about her telling. I wasn't a child and I wasn't going to be held against my will.

I had all my things stuffed into three large suitcases and began dragging them down the stairs as Maria followed behind me. If I wasn't in such a hurry I'd find those brass knuckles and clock her upside her head a few times. I didn't trust the bitch so I kept her in my peripheral. She was sneaky like that.

Ava must have been nervous as hell because she pulled up to the house faster than I thought she would have and jumped out the car. I came out with two of my suitcases and instructed her to get the other two. She was looking at me like I was crazy.

"We have a lot of catching up to do......Later!" I said motioning for her to get my other suitcase. I had enough time to run back upstairs for more it didn't look like Dollar would be coming back right away. "I'll be right back," I told my best friend passing her up and running in the house to load a couple trash bags with my shoes and handbags. Wasn't any need for me to leave them there hell I wasn't coming back. I glanced over at the closet. I'd watched dollar put money in a safe inside of it many nights when he thought I was sleeping. I had memorized the combination. I skipped over there 27-13-2 pop! Opened right up. I took the neat stacks of money and threw them in the trash bag too. That was peanuts to the pain and suffering he had just inflicted upon me I laughed to myself.

I could hear Maria whispering on the phone. "You favorite girl leaving right now!" she said. That bitch ratted me out. I put some pep in my step dragged them damn bags of shoes out to the car and threw them in the backseat. I was about to run back in the house and punch that hoe in the face for snitching but I could hear the screeching of tires coming around the corner.

"Shit!" I called out as I ran to the passenger side of the car and jumped in telling Ava to, "Go! Go! Go!"

One thing about my girl she might have asked a million questions but she was street smart and she knew shit wasn't right and we had to do it moving. She was cursing like hell as we sped off with Dollar honking behind us for her to stop.

"Bitch what the fuck you done got me in?!" she screamed yoking her way in and out of traffic.

I didn't answer the question I just continued to coach her to drive. We had to shake him. I didn't know what he was going to do and I wasn't trying to find out. I gave her the best overview of the situation I could after she told me she was going to stop the damn car if I didn't answer her question. The look she gave me if her eyes were knives I'd be cut into little bitty pieces.

"I have fucking kids Lauren!" she yelled at me just as Dollar rammed into the back her car. "And this nigga is fucking up my shit!!!!!" she hollered.

I didn't mean to get her into no shit but she was the only person I could call. How else would I have gotten out of that damn house if it wasn't for her? I didn't have anyone else to call. Brooke wasn't answering her phone probably sleeping off a night of partying.

"He's a pimp!" I said out of breath.

All hell broke loose in that car when I said that. I almost thought Ava was going to put that car in park and whoop my ass her damn self. She kept asking me what the fuck I was doing living in a pimps house. Why would she ask me such a stupid ass question? It was obvious what I was doing in his house. He was helping me get money. What did she want me to say it? Well I wasn't going to say shit because it was a temporary thing that I had to do for my family but she didn't need to know all of that.

"Lauren what the hell do you have going on?" Ava asked in a firmer tone.

She wasn't about the let it go at least not while I was in her car so I had to come clean. I let it all go every single detail omitting what had happened with Kat and the other two at the club. She stared at the road ignoring the blares of horns and the near miss we'd just had with a rusty brown car. I was impressed, my girl could drive.

"You been helping somebody rob banks?" I laughed to lighten up the mood looking back and noticing for the first time Dollar hadn't been following us anymore. Ava didn't answer she kept her eyes on the road as she made a turn into the neighborhood. "What are we coming over here for?" I asked sucking my teeth.

Every time something happened her, Brooke and sometimes even I would come to this spot. It was our safe haven. It was where we all had grown up and where Brooke's family still lived. It was early in the evening and as always there was a group of niggas hanging out front. Ava stepped out the car but I opted to stay in.

Whenever something went down they acted like they had to tell Chaz everything. He wasn't my man never was. Yeah he always looked out for me but that was beside the point. It was none of his damn business what I had been doing and I didn't have to tell him shit. I watched Ava disappear into the house she was gone for several minutes before Chaz emerged and headed towards the car.

He opened up the car door before he could say a word I opened my mouth, "Look I don't need to hear no shit from you," I said with my arms folded and a stank attitude.

He looked at me like I was crazy. "I'm not coming out here to talk to you," he said with just as much attitude as I had. His face turned up like he smelled something funky.

He grabbed Ava's purse and headed back in the house. No he didn't just come outside and not even speak to me or ask if I was okay. Chaz had never done me like that. I didn't know what his problem was but I for damn sure wasn't about to sit up there and let him just walk in the house and leave me outside looking stupid. I hopped out the car to go follow him. He turned and told me I needed to wait in the car. He gave me the coldest stare making me not even want to go inside the house.

I stopped in my tracks and stared him down at that point, finally feeling the disgrace I'd caused by selling my body the way I had. He hadn't looked at me like he was mad but disappointed, disgusted, hurt. Maybe he did think highly of me but who the fuck was he to judge me when he was out in these streets everyday doing whatever it was that he did. He had no room to look down on me. I did what I had to do just like he did.

The more I talked to myself the angrier I became with him. Ava running her ass in there telling them all my business like she was Ms. Polly Perfect. That bitch was sleeping with a married man no matter how she tried to slice that pie her man still had a wife. She was trying to call me a whore. Hell no I wasn't going to be standing outside. I maneuvered my way through the crowd that was gathered around the entrance of the house and stepped in.

The smell of weed smoke reeked throughout the entire place as I fanned my way through a haze of clouds. Just walking through there for those couple of seconds had me getting a contact. I coughed a little bit squeezing my way through the house looking for Ava and Chaz. I finally found them in the kitchen speaking in a low tone I couldn't quite make out what they were saying.

"If ya'll mothafuckas going to be talking about me you can at least do it in my presence!" I barked knowing they were discussing my little situation.

Both of them turned to stare at me Ava wore an irritated look on her face. I wanted to cuss her out friend or not. Nobody told her to be spreading my business around. "Talk about you for what?" Ava said walking up on me.

I really hoped she'd think long and hard about her next move because we would lose our friendship that day I was not in the mood. I didn't feel threatened she hadn't even come to me in a threatening way I just wasn't in the mood.

"Ohhhh bitch really," I said adding to the theatrics by changing my voice, bobbing my head, and throwing my arms around in the air. "You telling Chaz my business like he can do something about it!" I said looking down at her. She looked pregnant. I'd ask her a little later but right now the situation at hand was all about me.

"I didn't tell Chaz your mothafuckin' business," she barked. She had always been the little feisty one. She looked as if she was about to say something but then just brushed it off. "Matter of fact get your shit out my car and find somebody else to take you where you need to fuckin' go I got my own damn problems!" she added throwing her hands in the air and brushing past me. Next thing I knew she was back with Monsta and DeCorey lugging my shit into the kitchen.

I was going to say something to her ass but I thought better of it. She was my best friend the same best friend who had dropped everything she was doing to come get me when I needed her. I knew I could be selfish but not that selfish. I was still mad at her for telling my business but eventually everyone was going to find out anyway.

"Brooke will come to get you later," she told me as she walked past me avoiding eye contact. She was still mad as hell. "I've got things to do." She added walking towards the door.

I stood there not saying a word. When she walked out I turned to face Chaz he wasn't paying me any mind. I had to find someone to have an attitude with so I started in on him. "What the hell you got an attitude for?" I asked sliding into the squeaking brass chair with the dirty cushion in the kitchen.

"Lauren come on I'm not worried about you," he responded with his face scrunched. "You're a grown ass woman whatever it is you doing that got you paranoid you do it because you want to do it and that baby girl ain't any of my business."

Yeah he was mad that was cute. I didn't know how much Ava had told him but he knew something otherwise he wouldn't have an attitude with me. I was about to say something smart when Chaz's eyes lit up. Turning to look behind me I saw Tamica Anthony walking in.

What the hell? Really? I never could stand that bitch. Was he serious? He greeted her with a big hug that swallowed her small body right on up with a kiss to the forehead. They were talking and carrying on like I wasn't even sitting up in that bitch. I sat there staring at them with my arms folded. I caught eye contact with Chaz and rolled my eyes he laughed and kept on with his little show squeezing Tamica ratchet ass booty.

I wasn't about to sit in there and watch him with that bitch in my face. He knew we had history and that bitch had given me more trouble than a little bit and he had this bitch all caked up in my face. He was sho right. But regardless of what I

126

was going through I wasn't about to sit down and watch him with her. I stood up throwing my handbag over my shoulder and headed through the house bumping my way through the crowd of niggas down the steps outside the door.

I looked down at my phone damn my mother had been blowing it up. I opted not to call until Brooke got there and I was on my way. I knew I was going to get an earful and the way things had been going all day it wasn't no telling how I would respond to her verbal assault. I placed the phone back in my purse and continued walking down the street. I needed to get me a pack of cigarettes.

It had been a long time since I'd had a Newport but I needed something to calm my nerves. I bent the corner and strolled the two blocks down the street to the little store on the corner.

"Fie dolla turty seven cent please," the small Indian man behind the counter said. I shot him a ten dollar bill and kept it moving. I had to hurry up and get the hell out of that store he was funky as hell. His food was stinking too he had some type of curry vegetables or something. Whatever it was with the mixture of his funk and the dirt inside the store had my stomach turning.

I started my short walk back to the projects. I felt like I was in a horror flick or something because all of a sudden I got a nervous feeling as if I was being watched. I started to walk a little faster until I was at a slow trot. I whipped my head around to see who was behind me.

Damn I was trippin'. Nobody was following me. I looked down at my watch Brooke should have been pulling up at any minute. I looked up noticing a black car with dark tinted windows riding past me. The car looked familiar. I entered into the projects right before I could make it to the front door of apartment 6913 Dollars car skid into a parking stall in front of me.

I was frozen in time. He jumped out the car and it was like everything was moving in slow motion. I let out a scream and took off running as fast as I could. He was in my neck of the woods I could maneuver through those projects and shake him. I looked back to see how much space we had between us. Losing my balance I crashed into the ground face first. I lay there for a moment dazed and confused.

When I finally mustered enough energy to scramble to my feet Dollar was right up on me with that menacing look on his face. I screamed as he dragged me back to his car.

# AVA

## (14)

The day had turned out more exciting than I had anticipated. The shit with Lauren was crazy. I never did understand how she always got herself in those types of situations but she did and somebody always had to come bail her ass out. My car was fucked up! What the hell was she thinking messing around with some guerilla pimp? You would think the older she got the wiser she became. When it came to Lauren the older she got the less common sense she had.

I had too many problems of my own to be getting caught up in her mess. On my way home I'd called Cameron and told him about my drama filled afternoon. He was pissed to say the least. I had never heard him talk like that. He told me to stay away from Lauren because he couldn't have me or our baby getting hurt because of her negligence. He went on and on about me having as less stress as possible while I carried our child.

I couldn't blame him though he was right. As much as I loved Lauren I couldn't put myself in harms' way she'd have to handle her business on her own. I was going to call the police or drive right down to the police station with him on our tail but she was adamant about not doing so. I could read between the lines she was hiding something. Our old neighborhood was the only place I could take her and feel comfortable about leaving her there. Shaking my head I rubbed lotion on my small belly.

Ashley didn't live too far from my home and I was excited about spending an evening relaxing and being pampered. I wasn't going to be able to drink but I was sure I'd have a good time. That would give me an opportunity to fill my sister in on everything that was going on in my life and let her know that I was pregnant.

I listened to Mary J. Blige on the way over. Her voice was so soothing and every word she sang I could relate to. She was the ghetto diva's voice. The hood chick turned classy lady spokeswoman. I couldn't sing to save my life but I belted out the words to My Life like I'd signed a contract of my own. Music was most definitely good for the soul. When I pulled up to Ashley's house none of the other ladies were there. I had come early so I could help her set things up for the night.

I parked behind Ash's car and walked up to the hard oak door with the stained glass in the middle. Ringing the doorbell I waited for Ashley to answer. When she opened the door I smiled. I hadn't seen my sister in quite some time and she was looking great. Her skin glowed and her hair was long thick and flowing.

"Uh oh!" I said smiling running my fingers through her soft straight hair.

She twirled around giggling asking me if I liked her new hairdo. I loved it. She had always had long naturally curly hair. She finally took my advice and got a keratin treatment done to soften and straighten it out. She looked good. More sophisticated even. My baby sister was growing up. I remembered when I'd met her for the first time. We clicked instantly. It was like the bloodline we shared brought us together immediately.

It didn't matter that her mother was white and our father chose to abandon me and take care of her. I knew that we would grow to love each other like sisters did. She was the only person that I had a relationship with on that side of the family including my dad. He hated that for whatever reason maybe he hated my mother maybe he hated himself for cheating on his wife hell I was sure he hated me for being born. Whatever the case may have been it didn't hold any weight when it came to my sister and I.

When she was off at college I made sure she had nice school clothes and a few dollars in her pocket. I couldn't do much but what I could do she appreciated and always talked about how she would get the chance to repay me. I didn't need repayment. The only thing I needed was for my Ashley to succeed and never make the same mistakes I did. So far so good she was an amazing attorney, owned a beautiful home and a car, wore nice clothes, had a nice little savings and was still humble. My sister was a good spirited woman. Although I was only a little less than a year old than her I still held on to that big sister title with pride.

"You're early!" she smiled closing the door behind me.

"Of course I am," I responded shrugging. "You know I wasn't going to let you decorate by yourself."

As she talked I zoned in on a familiar face sitting on the sofa in her living room. Everything Ashley was saying fell on deaf ears. I stared at the woman sitting in my sister's living room with her hair pulled back in a high bun. Her skin was either absolutely flawless or she had on a ton of makeup that even Mary Kay would be ashamed of.

Her eyes pierced through me like daggers but I didn't back down regardless of what her relationship was with my sister that was still my sister and figuratively speaking she was now on my turf. Ashley darted around the room jumping from one idea to the next while I stood directly in front of the woman eyeing her down and she doing the same.

"Oh my God!" Ashley screeched snapping me out of the stare down. "Ava this is a long time friend of mine Marteen," she said extending her hand out to me. "Marteen this is my sister Ava." She said introducing us.

When Marteen stood to shake my hand I noticed she no longer had a belly. Her abs lay flat underneath her jumpsuit. I gave her a little smile nodding my head and looking down at her belly before extending my hand.

"Nice to meet you Marteen," I said giving her a firm handshake.

She didn't back down. She smiled right back matching my handshake saying likewise. Ashley didn't feel the thickness of the tension that had began to fill the room. I felt as if I had the upper hand with her for the first time. She was always one step ahead of me except for this time. This time she was taken by surprise. She didn't have time to lie about being pregnant or plan her little attack on my character.

"So ladies," Ashley said clasping her hands together still oblivious to the fact that Marteen and I most definitely had a problem. "We don't have much to do we have about an hour and half to get everything ready for the par-," she said trailing off as she looked from Marteen and back to me.

"Is everything okay?" she asked with a look of disapproval look on her face.

"Of course," I responded shaking my head never taking my eyes off of Marteen. The more I looked at her the more I wanted to slap her down but I would respect my sisters' home. If she only knew the things I did about her crazy ass friend Marteen. I am sure she knew I would be telling Cameron about her little lie and just to make sure she didn't try to weasel her way out of what she had coming I snapped a picture with my phone.

"What the hell!" Marteen said shielding herself from the blinding light of the camera.

"I'm sorry," I said pretending to give a damn about her being mad I caught her in a lie. "I love capturing memories." I said with a fake smile.

Ashley looked from Marteen to me and back to Marteen again. "Am I missing something?" she inquired.

"Not at all," Marteen said quickly gathering her purse. "I really have to go I just realized I have to take care of something," she said rushing towards the door.

Ashley rushed behind her asking if she would make it back. Marteen told her she would try but she couldn't guarantee it. I laughed on the inside. She must have realized that she didn't have that fake ass belly wrapped around her waist. Wait until I showed Cameron the picture I'd just taken.

Ashley turned to me with a confused look on her face and I just shrugged my shoulders. "I know you're not telling me something," she stated in a matter of fact tone. "You'll let me know before the night is over." She said joining me at the window as we watched Ashley scurry to her car that was parked across the street.

How did I not notice that before I walked in? I could have prepared myself a little better I thought to myself. Oh well the picture I'd just snapped was good enough. I wondered where she was headed. Probably to plot some more but then again what leg did she have to stand on. It was apparent she was on the losing team. Not that I was playing games but she clearly was.

Ashley and I got the house together just as her guests started to arrive. She had a nice spread. Fresh fruit tray with strawberries, pineapple, mango, cherries, kiwi, and any fruit other you wanted spread neatly on trays, there was wine and other finger foods as well. We had laughed when we were putting things together. We were like night and day she had fillet mignon and I preferred smothered pork chops. We were so different but yet so alike.

That ladies night was exactly what I needed by the time all the festivities were over with I was feeling like I hadn't felt in quite some time. That massage I received was on point. That man worked out kinks I didn't even know I had. I was definitely going to start getting massages more often. I felt like I was floating on air. When my head hit that pillow I was surely going to be out for the count.

It didn't take long to help Ashley get her home back in order after all of the other ladies left so we sat around and talked for a little while. I couldn't keep my secret any longer. I told my sister I was pregnant again.

"I know," she said nonchalantly.

Looking at her like she was crazy I asked, "How do you know I'm pregnant?"

"Honey, I am paid to know," she said smiling. "Plus you haven't had an alcoholic beverage all night and I know how you love your alcohol and your pooch is a little larger," she added poking me in the belly. "Now you're glowing!"

"You're one nosey ass broad!" I teased laughing as I popped a strawberry into my mouth.

"Girl you are crazy," my sister said slapping me on my shoulder.

I know I am wrong but I needed to get some information out of my sister. So I threw out the bait. "So what's up with your girl Marteen?" I asked.

My sister gave me the all knowing look. "I don't know about that girl," she started. "She's been acting really funny lately."

We talked for a little while and the most I got from my sister is that they had been friends since elementary school. Marteen came from a family with money and supposedly her father had ties to the mafia. According to Ashley it was only rumors of course. From what I understood Marteen was a spoiled little rich girl who always got her way. She'd been questioned regarding the disappearance of a classmate when they were in high school but nothing ever became of it. Ashley said her father just made the situation for Marteen "go away". My sister had her reservations.

The more I heard about Cameron's wife the more I was starting to wish I had waited until their divorce was over and she had moved on. I mean from the sounds of things she had several screws loose for a lack of better words. I didn't need those types of problems in my life. It was getting late and I promised the kids we would get up early the following morning go out for breakfast and enjoy the spring weather maybe go to the zoo or something.

I gave Ashley a big hug and started my journey home. I called Cameron to ask him if he would be stopping by that night he didn't answer so I left a message for him to give me a call back. I noticed a police car behind me flashing its lights. I slowly pulled over reaching in my glove compartment to get out my insurance and registration and was fumbling through my purse for my driver's license.

The officer walked up to my car shining his light through my window. I squinted to see behind the bright light as I handed over my documentation. Suddenly my door flung open and I was being snatched out of the car. I had seen too many people get their ass whooped for resisting arrest so I allowed myself to be manhandled asking what I had done wrong.

When the cop twirled me around and slammed my back against my car I was instantly filled with fear. I recognized the face. I didn't know what I had done to have this man on my ass like this but I was sure to find out now. Remember me? He asked eyes wide snarling like some type of animal.

"What do you want?" I asked timidly reaching inside my handbag for my pistol. As he loosened his grip on my shoulders and gave me a couple inches of space I slammed my knee into his groin and took off running down the street. I could hear him screaming shit as he doubled over. I wasn't about to turn around to see where he was at, all I knew was I had to get out of sight and fast. I wasn't taking any chances.

I had my gun but what the hell would that look like me shooting a police officer who pulled me over? I was in enough shit. I didn't need to be battling an entire police force fighting for my life. Running was my best option at that point.

I hide inside some bushes on the side of a dark house. Go figure I would take this way home tonight through a neighborhood full of dilapidated homes that had been boarded up for years. I peeked through a small opening in the bushes to see where that psychotic ass cop was. I couldn't see shit. Damn! I cursed to myself. Feeling around quietly in my purse I searched with my hands for my cell phone.

I wanted to call 911 but it was a cop that was after me. Who the hell was I going to call now? As my mind raced my phone began to vibrate I answered whispering hello into the receiver.

"GOTCHA!" that crazy ass bastard yelled snatching me out of the bushes I dropped my phone and let out a loud scream. He was pulling me back to his squad car didn't know where he was taking me or what he planned on doing with me but I wasn't going out without a fight.

Out of nowhere someone whipped past me and BANG! Knocked the hell out of my stalker. The hit sounded like a baseball bat hitting a ball for a homerun. He fell to the ground with a thud. I turned to see an old dirty woman in rags holding a metal pipe in her hand. She smiled showing me rotten brown and black teeth. Pointing for me to get to my car.

I didn't have time to thank her. I would come back after I got to safety and make sure that she was okay. I didn't know why this man had been following me. I glanced at the cars tags and quickly memorized the sequence of numbers for future reference. Jumped in my ride and literally burned rubber getting the hell on.

Things were starting to get very interesting. I had been victimized enough over the past several months the old me was beginning to show her ugly head and it would most definitely be a different end to the story when these people came running up on me the next time. Reaching in my purse while keeping my eyes on the road I searched for my cell phone. It wasn't there.

I took my right hand dumping all the contents out on the seat next to me. Times like that I didn't need a big ass bag. "Shit!" I cursed a loud I had dropped my phone in the bushes. My best bet was to make my way down to the police station. What if I ran into someone who was in on this? What if Marteen's father really was associated with the mafia and there was a hit out on me? I couldn't trust anyone. I needed to go home to check on my kids. Get them to my mother's house until I figured out exactly who was after me.

# MARTEEN

## (15)

Time was ticking, too much was going on and I had taken things too far to stop now. Of course if I wanted something done right I'd have to do it myself. Good thing I stayed back to make sure Chester did what he was supposed to do. As always he fell short wasn't aware of his surroundings and got his ass knocked out by the old homeless hag that was living in one of those abandoned houses.

I stayed back watching as Ava got away. I could read her like a book though. She wouldn't get far she'd run to the person she trusted most my husband and at that point it didn't matter because it was time for him to go too. He had caused me far too much grief. If he had just come back home to me like I told him everything would be going great. I could have gotten pregnant and I wouldn't have had to lie.

Good thing the street didn't have any traffic going down it. Ava had played right into my hand. I waited down the street from the Ashley's home for hours. The plan was to stop her put her in the cop car and take her to my parents lake house but hell when she made that detour down that empty street I had a change of plans. Just kill the bitch put her in one of those houses and get it over with. I was going to head back to Ashley's to make sure I had an alibi but opted against it. That was the best move I'd made in a long time.

I sat in my car contemplating my next move as I watched Chester's big ass hit the ground. He never saw it coming but that old homeless bitch had did me a favor because when it was all said and done I was getting rid of his ass too. I'd done it before but now I was older, wiser, and stronger now it wouldn't be as hard to rid myself of anyone who posed a threat to my cause. I sighed as I got out of my car and quickly ran towards the old woman pretending to be a concerned citizen. No witnesses were all that was going through my head.

This woman wasn't a spring chicken she backed as far away from me as she could. I spoke slow and deliberate as I attempted to approach her. I just needed to get up on her so I could zap her with my stun gun subdue her and get Chester's ass up so we could handle her and find Ava. She looked afraid like she knew something that I didn't know. Ava had gotten away I wasn't about to let her get away too. My plan was unraveling right before my eyes and I couldn't have that. I needed to get this thing back on track.

I reached out to grab her. She jumped still holding the pipe she'd hit Chester with high in the air. I held my hands out pretending to come in peace. Her eyes darted from left to right as she backed away looking for a place to run. There was no where she could go that I wouldn't find her. I just needed her to let her guard down well at least that pipe so I could get up on her. I knew I could overpower her and put an end to all of it. She didn't have much to live for anyway she was dirty and homeless living in an abandoned house.

"Ma'm, I'm here to help you," I lied taking small steps towards her.

She continued to back away shaking her head. I was sick of playing games with this woman. She had put a monkey wrench in my plans I wasn't taking it lightly. She didn't have anything to live for clearly so why was she so worried about what the hell was going on with anyone else. She needed to mind her own damn business maybe she wouldn't have gotten herself in such a sticky situation.

"You have nowhere to go," I said finally fed up with her little game of cat and mouse.

"Ms. Marteen?" she said squinting to get a better look at me. "I know you," she said pointing and shaking her head looking me directly into my eyes. "Dear God," she said weeping. I had never seen that woman a day in my life. It was obvious that she however knew me. I couldn't place where. I stepped in closer trying to get a good look at her face through all the dirt and grime and her matted hair. She continued to step backwards causing herself to stumble over the curb. My mind raced back in time and in an instance I realized exactly who she was.

*There was nothing on earth that I couldn't have as a young teenage girl except Lorenzo Banks. I'd done everything I could to get his attention but it was never enough for him. He put all his attention in his little cheerleading ass girlfriend Alexis. She wasn't prettier than me she didn't have as much money as me and she didn't love him the way I did. She bounced her big ass around in front of all the boys. Wearing those short skirts and smiling in everyone's faces. She didn't have anything that I didn't have.*

*I presented myself with class. I didn't have to wear cheap ass short skirts. My entire outfit probably cost what her poor ass single mother spent in renting that raggedy ass apartment they lived in. She was nothing* compared to me and yet he was with her. I hated her for that and when I tried to convince him that he should be with me and not with her he laughed at me like what I was saying was some kind of joke to him. It hurt my feelings but I didn't give up after all he didn't say no.

Every party he went to I was there and that night I got him drunk he took my virginity. It was the most beautiful experience I'd ever had. I approached his locker that Monday morning and wrapped my arms around his waist from behind. He turned to see it was me and frowned looking around to make sure no one had seen. I couldn't understand why he was acting like that. I stood on my tip toes trying to kiss him and he moved away pushing me back. Told me I was making a fool of myself asking me what my problem was.

I told him he did love me otherwise he wouldn't have taken my virginity. He laughed at me again telling me I was making a fool of myself again and that I needed to pull myself together. I didn't mean anything to him and it shouldn't have happened it was a mistake. I was a mistake. Lorenzo said that I needed to keep my mouth shut so things wouldn't get back to Alexis. I tried to reason with him but he ignored me. I tried to blackmail him and that was when he threatened to kick my ass. He told me all the money in the world couldn't make me Alexis and I needed to leave him alone and walked away.

I stood in that hallway all alone tears falling down my face. How dare he speak to me like that. I would tell my father that he raped me that would show him to speak to me in that manner. I would kill him and his precious little Alexis. Yeah that was what I planned to do. As I watched him walk away though I couldn't bring myself to rid the earth of his presence so my thoughts roamed back to Alexis. She thought she was so much prettier than me. She thought she was something special. I was going to show her ass she was nothing special at all.

I invited her to my house after school one day. I'd pretended to be interested in learning some moves so I could participate in the cheer tryouts coming up. She was just so gullible Ms. Goodie Two Shoes always trying to help someone always talking about becoming a doctor so she could cure *people of cancer. That bitch wasn't shit but a whore. Always trying to help out the needy but I didn't need her she needed me more than I needed her. She came to the LeBlanc Estate as planned. We practiced cheering for what seemed like forever.*

*The whole time Alexis reminding me to smile and let her hear some excitement. What the hell was there to be smiling or excited about? It wasn't like I was getting a new piece of jewelry or something. After we finished our so called practice I asked her if she was hungry and had our maid and nanny Delores make us lunch. Delores had worked for our family for as long as I could remember. She was the only mother I ever had. She was my comforter. When I was sick she took care of me, when I got hurt she dried away my tears, when I was happy I shared that with her.*

*At first I wanted to poison Alexis but I hated that bitch so much I needed to get up close and personal. We sat in my room flipping through magazines talking about absolutely nothing I was interested in. I was looking for something that was attractive about her personality. I'd come up with nothing. Maybe Lorenzo loved having sex with her.*

*"You're skins so beautiful," I said to her rubbing my hand down her arm as we sat on the bed. She shied away a little but that was okay my plan was set in motion. I switched the conversation back to the girls in the magazine we were flipping through talking about modeling and how they looked so perfect but us regular girls were far prettier because we didn't need makeup artists to make us beautiful it came naturally. She agreed.*

*I moved on to talking about breasts and asses and started my game telling her I was a 36C naturally but I wanted smaller breast. She wasn't uncomfortable with the conversation until I took off my shirt and bra exposing my perky breasts and told her to feel them. All of a sudden she began to gather her things and wanted to leave. I apologized for making her feel uncomfortable and asked her to please stay. She said she really had to go but she wasn't walking out of that bedroom.*

*I quickly stood in front of her apologizing once again forcing her to look into my eyes. It was something about my eyes that always seemed to mesmerize people. She hesitated for a millisecond but that was all I needed to make my move. I pressed myself up against her pinning her up against the wall letting my lips barely touch her neck. She put her hands against me trying to push me back but I whispered to her that it was ok. She was tense. I told her how beautiful I thought she was and how I couldn't help myself as my tongue trailed on her neck then sucked softly.*

*She said she wasn't into this type of thing and she had a boyfriend. I assured her I wasn't there to hurt her. I urged her to relax as I slipped my hand up skirt and parted her lips with my finger rubbing her clit as she allowed a moan to escape her lips. I'd never had a lesbian encounter before wasn't into women at all but this was all for the greater good. It was all a part of the plan. She whispered for me to please stop but she didn't want me to stop I could tell by how wet she was. I continued to go on exposing her breast and licking them.*

*I did things to her like I'd watched on those porn movies my parents thought they could hide from me. I think I made her cum. When it was all over with she lay on top of my bed crying. She said that I had raped her. The nerve of her to insinuate such a thing when she enjoyed every last second of it, I told her she liked it she came back with I told you to stop. That's what her mouth said that wasn't what her body said. She said she was going to tell. I couldn't let her do that. I did the only thing I knew to do the only thing I really wanted to do I snatched the letter opener from my desk and sliced her with it. I had only planned to scare her at that point. I wanted to play my game a little longer before I let her have it but she ruined that.*

*She wouldn't stop screaming and crying so I continued to cut her over and over again and then stabbing her until I heard nothing more but the gargling sound of her choking on her own blood. I stood there with the weapon in my hand looking down at her out of breath. She wasn't so pretty anymore I thought tilting my head to the side. Matter of fact she was ugly. There was blood everywhere on my walls, my comforter was soaked, and my face and hands were covered with crimson red. I sniffed and wiped my nose.*

*I hadn't even heard my parents come home. I was in a daze. I don't even know how long I stood there looking at her lie there her eyes looking directly into mine. They were empty though. I had literally watched her life leave her body. There was fear etched in them. Fear caused by me Ms. Marteen LeBlanc and that made me powerful. More beautiful than she was and I was in control there was nothing she could do about it. My father burst through my door as he normally did to see how my day had went as I stood there with the letter opener in my hand staring at my victim.*

*He screamed at me asking me what had I done. I don't believe I answered him. That was the first time I saw my father cry. My mother rushed upstairs and they were acting as if the world had ended. The world was just beginning for me. That was when I knew it wasn't in my head I could have whatever I wanted in life and I had the power to give and to take it away just like that. My father called Delores the housekeeper up to the room to clean things up and she started acting dramatic. They covered up my sins that day. Daddy paid Delores a large lump sum to keep her mouth shut but soon she just disappeared. Alexis' body was never found it was buried on the estate property in the family graveyard that lay just north of the guest house.*

I'd always wondered where Delores had gone. She had damn near raised me and she disappeared on me. For a long time she was the only parental figure I had ever had. My parents were always too busy for me. After all those years I was standing face to face with her. She was standing right in front of me a tattered old woman living in an abandoned home. Fate would have it she had to face her past one day. There I was in the flesh standing there right before her eyes.

"Ms. Delores?" I said reaching out to her.

She continued to back away. She was acting as if I had the plague or something. This woman had to know that I loved her. I didn't want to hurt Ms. Delores she had saved me from a life full of grief. Why had she left our home? She didn't have to live like this. A part of me I had buried long ago was coming out at the sight of this woman this angel that was back in my life. She kept her eyes locked on me but didn't say a word. I wanted to help her she looked afraid.

Why should I help her when she had abandoned me? She left me with *them* all alone I had no one after she left.

"You left me Ms. Delores," I said. "I've missed you," tears began to roll down my face. That woman had raised me not my parents and she just walked away all because of one mistake I'd made. I was tormented should I be mad or happy that I found her again. She'd always nurtured me and loved me.

POP! A loud sound pierced the air and Ms. Delores went flying back into the yard of one of the deteriorating houses. I screamed *Noooo!* I rushed to her side kneeling down I thanked God she had only been grazed but the old woman was knocked out cold. Chester came running up towards us. I stood up and began pounding him in the chest calling him every name but a child of God. He was so stupid. He allowed me to beat him as he pulled me up the street to my car and told me we had to get the hell out of there. The gunshot was going to bring the police.

"Chester I'm not leaving Ms. Delores here she is hurt!" I shouted. "Help me get her in my car now!" I demanded. He stood there with a confused look on his face until I reiterated with a loud NOW! I didn't have time to explain to his dumb ass and I told him just that. He did as he was told scooping her into his arms and to my car. I drove down the dark street and into the night heading towards my house. Picking up my phone

I made a quick call. With a sigh of relief I focused on the road. Someone would be meeting me there to help Ms. Delores.

# CAMERON

## (16)

I was worried sick breaking every driving law there was trying to get to Ava's house. When I got there Ava wasn't home neither were the kids. I had tried to call her several times but couldn't get through. I didn't know what the hell was going on but I needed to know that Ava was okay. My mind was going a hundred miles a minute I didn't know where to start. I realized I had Dominique's cell phone number saved in my phone. I held my breath as I waited for an answer.

"Hello?" she said.

"Hey baby girl," I said trying to sound cool. The truth was my heart was beating out of my chest. I was panicking damn near about to pass out.

"Hey Cam!" she said excitedly. "Mama it's Cam!" she yelled into the phone.

Thank God for small favors hearing Ava's voice in the background was music to my ears. She excused Dominique and whispered into the phone. I could tell she was crying she was talking so fast I couldn't make out a word she was saying. I had to tell her to slow down.

"Cameron I am so scared," was all I could make out between her sobs. "What the hell is going on?" she asked as if I had the secret. I didn't even know what had happened but I remained calm.

"Ok, babe start from the beginning," I said.

She ran down how she was headed home from her sisters' ladies night party when a police officer stopped and attacked her. It all sounded crazy I had her repeat the story twice until she became angry. I had to assure her I didn't think she was lying I just wanted to make sure that I was understanding what she was telling me.

"Cameron please get here I'm scared," she cried. I could hear her voice trembling. I knew she wasn't lying. I didn't know why any of this was happening but as her man I was going to find out come hell or high water. I hated to go back to the old me but times like that required me to step back and become that other dude.

I headed to Ava's mothers house to pick her up. We decided that the kids needed to sleep over there for a few nights until we could figure out what the hell was happening and why. I had called a few of my old acquaintances but the streets weren't talking. Ava had even made a couple phone calls of her own. Seemed to be we knew some of the same people.

When I pulled up to her mother's house she was already standing outside waiting for me. As she got in the car she said, "Cameron, I dropped my phone in the bushes," as she stared at me from the passenger side of the car.

I didn't want to go back to where she said everything had gone down. The police could be swarming the area by now and I didn't want to answer any questions I didn't want her answering any either especially with a dead cop laying face first on the pavement. She insisted that we at least needed to drive past just to see if anyone was there.

When we reached the avenue it was dark as hell on that street. Not a police car in sight and no big ass cop laying on the ground either.

"Are you sure this is where it happened?" I asked suspiciously.

"I know what the hell I'm talking about Cam!" she snapped. "I'm not crazy like your wife!" she added. That had come out of nowhere but I guess I had that coming. She had been under a lot of pressure lately. I needed to just listen to her so we could move on. I didn't say a word as I parked the car on the side of the curb and turned off the engine.

"She's not pregnant you know?" she added with a loud sigh.

"Ava what are you talking about?" I said taking my thumb and forefinger massaging the bridge of my nose.

"Marteen," she said. "She's my sisters divorce lawyer. Ashley Christensen attorney at law. I saw your wife tonight and there was no belly." She stated. "I took a picture of her with my phon-." Her words trailed off as if she'd had an epiphany. "She left that party early so she could set me up!" she shrieked.

I knew Marteen was crazy but she wasn't that crazy. She had her issues but everybody had their issues. She would never do something like that.

"Ava," I said looking at her in disbelief.

"Oh what your precious wife can do no wrong huh?" she said with a slight chuckle. "Even after she shows up at my house twice showing her ass she still is the picture perfect woman to you." She said tears now flowing.

Ava was putting word in my mouth that was not what I meant. I knew that Marteen could be over the top a lot of times but try to physically harm someone I couldn't wrap my mind around that. I didn't say a word as Ava went on her tirade.

"You know what Cam I just want to find my phone and you can take me back to my mother's house," she said slamming the door as she exited.

She walked right over to the bushes and picked up her phone. Well at least I knew she didn't make that up. As we headed back to the car I looked down at the ground and noticed what looked like a small pool of blood on the pavement. Ava continued walking to the car leaving me behind as I investigated the scene. Something had happened but I didn't believe Marteen was the cause of it all.

I jogged back to the car and started the engine. I didn't want to fight with Ava I tried to make small talk but she didn't say a word she sat there fumbling that phone in between in her fingers. She was trembling. I wasn't for sure if it was from fear or anger. Either way I didn't like seeing her feel that way so I opted to apologize. Tried to plead my case get her to see things the way I saw them but she cut me off telling me she didn't want to talk about it anymore.

She asked me to pull over to a gas station so she could get something to drink. When she got out the car she left her phone sitting on the seat. There was a picture of Marteen on the screen with no sign of being pregnant. Her small round stomach was gone. Her hair pulled back in a ponytail her MAC face impeccable. I jerked back in the seat shaking my head. I couldn't put anything past that woman I'd said I do to. She'd made such a fuss about being pregnant with our child and it was a bold faced lie.

The longer I knew that woman the more I couldn't stand her. What was she going to do when I found out she wasn't really pregnant? She thought she was so smart but never thought anything through that's why she always had people like her father cleaning up her mess. He'd do anything for that little girl all dressed up like the perfect woman. Maybe they had hired someone on the police force to hurt Ava so I would come back to her. At this point I wasn't putting anything past them. There was a time when I was called to their home to give a man medical treatment. That man was paid off a large lump sum to keep his mouth shut about what? I don't know didn't have anything to do with me.

I wasn't aware of the whole story and no one had given me the entire truth about the situation but it didn't sit well with me but I helped because she was my wife. I remember the look in that mans eyes he was fearful. I did as I was asked and kept my mouth shut didn't ask any questions. Where I came from the more you know the more expendable you became. I wasn't a witness to anything but helping out a friend of the family that was it. I wanted to keep it that way. Mr. LeBlanc had a lot of ties to a lot of people many organizations. People who could make you or break you literally.

I respected the LeBlanc's and had always played my position accordingly. However, when it came down to protecting my seed and those that I loved I didn't give a damn who they were affiliated with I would put on my soldier gear and go hard for mine. I prayed that Marteen wasn't behind this bullshit but my gut was telling me that she was knee deep in this shit. I couldn't allow her to terrorize the woman who was carrying my child hell the woman I loved and planned to marry in the future. If I had to go to war and lose everything I had worked so hard to obtain I would. No questions asked.

Ava quietly got back in the car putting on her seat belt. I started to drive off without saying anything but I couldn't I needed her to know that things were good and I believed her.

"I believe you," I said looking at her waiting for a response.

"It doesn't even matter," she said taking a sip of her water. "Can you just take me to my mother's house?" she asked sighing.

She was angry with me I understood that but she was going to have to talk to me. Things weren't just going to go away. I knew she had left that picture up for me to take a look. I felt bad that I had to have proof to believe her. I knew Marteen had been giving her hell for quite some time and I still had continued to give Marteen the benefit of the doubt. I wasn't in love with Marteen anymore but I did have some love for her even after everything we'd been through. We had a child together.

"Ava come on stop acting like that," I pleaded sincerely. We weren't about to have drama because of someone else.

"Stop what?" Ava said whipping her head around in classic sista girl fashion. "Listen, why don't you stop putting that bitch on a fuckin' pedestal. I know what the fuck happened to me tonight I could have died I have three other kids to take care of. And you are talking about a psychotic bitch like she can do no wrong. I know what I'm feeling and that bitch is trying to hurt me. I tell you what though," she said pulling a big ass gun out of her purse. "I will kill that bitch before she kills me she won't catch me slipping again."

Ava had gotten really gangster. All I could do was look at her in amazement. My eyes darted back and forth from the road, to the gun, to her face for several seconds. She was not playing and I really couldn't blame her. She had to protect herself. I chose to remain silent the rest of the ride until we got to her mother's house.

Before we got up to the door it flung open Mrs. Tanner standing there in her nightgown urging us to come in looking from side to side before she slammed the door shut and locked it. I looked at the side of the door and noticed a shotgun leaning against the wall. What in the hell?

"A pig came here looking for you," she said nodding towards Ava with a cigarette hanging out of her mouth. "I thought you were done with that entire hood shit girl a long time ago," she said shaking her head from side to side eyeing Ava down.

Ava gave me a look that said it all.

"This is very important mom," she said. "What did he look like?"

Mrs. Tanner went on to describe the man that had been following Ava for quite some time which also happened to be the man who had attacked her earlier that night. The more things unraveled the more everything became a mystery.

"I told that bastard if he didn't have a search warrant to get his ass off my property and he left," she said peeking between the blinds to make sure no one was outside. "I called down to the police station to find out what you had gotten yourself into nobody seems to know anything. You have no warrants. Nothing." She added with her lips pursed into a perfect o. Had things not been so serious the whole scene would have been comical.

"You got a gun?" her mother asked eyeing her daughter.

Ava pulled out her burner cocking it back putting one in the chamber. Her mother nodded. "Shoot first ask questions later I don't trust that mothafucka," she said with the cigarette still dangling from her lips.

"Listen mom I really need to go," her mother cut her off shooing us on and telling me to take care of her daughter and her grandbaby. We both looked back at her like how in the hell did she know Ava was pregnant we hadn't even told the kids yet. She assured us that a mother always knew it was her job to know.

I called my brother Kymani but he said he was a little tied up at the moment he would call me back. That nigga always had something going on he stayed busy. I told him that it couldn't wait I needed him to meet me at his spot ASAP and hung up on him. He tried to call me back but I kept sending his ass to voicemail. From the urgency in my voice I knew my big brother was going to drop what he was doing and come holler at me. I didn't need him often but when I did he knew it was serious. I zipped over to his house and waited in his driveway.

Moments later he pulled up looking like he'd been playing bumper cars. I jumped out the car leaving Ava asleep inside the car while I greeted my brother. "Damn," I said eyeing his ride. "What the hell happened to your car bro?" I said checking out all the damage putting my fist to my lips laughing.

155

"You know how it is," he said smiling that signature smile of his and giving me some dap. "Sometimes Dollars hoes get out of line and I have to straighten them back out." He said nodding towards the woman sitting in his car looking crazy as hell.

My brother was smart as hell I never could understand why he didn't channel that energy towards something positive. We had a wonderful mother she did everything she could to make sure her boys did something positive with their lives. I made it out the hood my brother he couldn't let the streets go.

He played on women's intelligence made them believe he gave a damn about them and then put them out on the hoe stroll. If they disobeyed him he let them know exactly who was boss. He was regulating women all the way back in elementary school. I loved the ladies but the ladies loved him and he preyed on that love. He used it against them and benefited from it. He made it out the hood alright but not because he did anything spectacular. Only because he was a predator.

I felt bad for the broad sitting in the car it looked like she'd had one hell of a day. I didn't want Ava to think I condoned that type of shit but I had to get my brothers help. My brother wasn't only a pimp he was a gangster too. He'd been out in the streets with the best of them hustling everything from women, to dope, to stolen merchandise. Women just happened to be his specialty. He made the most money with the least problems handling his hoes and he liked it that way.

Shaking my head I told him to be on his best behavior I had my other half with me we needed some help. My brother knew a lot of people he had connections. Many high ranking officials had been using his services for years. They considered him a friend. He'd done a lot of business with the mayor, senators, chief of police, hell the district attorney's office, just to name a few. If I knew anyone that could help it was definitely him. When I opened the door it startled Ava she jumped looking around taking in the atmosphere.

She jumped out the car going berserk.

"Awl hell fuckin' naw," she said in the most ghetto country ass tone I had ever heard. She turned to see my brothers face glanced at his car and went off some more. As she screamed and hollered threatening and going off I started putting two and two together. I'd be damned Dollar was the pimp that had been chasing her and her friend Lauren earlier. The day couldn't have gotten crazier. I looked back at my brother's car and it was rocking from side to side the woman in the car was screaming at the top of her lungs beating on the window.

My brother looked at me with a grin on his face. "Dollar, got the child locks on bitches always trying to run away," he said.

I didn't know what the hell to do shit was getting far too out of hand. Dollar was getting a kick out of everything that was unfolding I didn't see a damn thing funny about the situation. Here I was stuck in the middle of yet some more shit.

# AVA

## (17)

I know that crazy ass pimp is not my child's uncle! As soon as I opened my eyes and saw where I was at I knew that some bullshit was about to go down. It took less than three minutes to see Dollar or whatever the hell his name was with my best friend Lauren locked in his busted up Cadillac. It was about to go down I had my pistol on me now as bad of a night I was having somebody was getting shot today and I would faithfully go to jail. I'd had more than enough.

Lauren was going crazy in that car hair every damn where face all scraped up like she had gotten her ass drug and him the pimp named Dollar standing outside talking to Cameron laughing like something was cute. I wanted to shoot his ass for fucking up my car too. I knew I'd see his lame ass someday didn't know it would have been that day and for damn sure wasn't expecting him to be Cameron's brother.

"Let her out the damn car," I said walking up on a laughing Kymani aka Dollar the big bad ass pimp and pointing in his face. He just continued to laugh as Cameron looked confused. I knew one thing he'd better check his brother before I dug in my pocketbook. I walked around the pair and snatched at the latch to open the door. It was locked. Unlock the door I told a hysterical Lauren through the window. Every time she would pull up the lock for me Dollar would hit the lock button so I couldn't open the door.

I stared back at Cameron waiting for him to do something. He spoke into Dollar's or whatever his name was ear and he walked over to the car and let Lauren out. She was jumping up and down and carrying on talking about how we had to get out of there. I mean I know the man had beat her up, pimp slapped her and some more shit but right now she needed to calm her ass down I had other shit that needed to be taken care of and I wasn't trying to hear what she was talking about. She shouldn't have gotten herself involved with a pimp in the first damn place.

"Lauren," I said calmly. "Chill the hell out we have business to take care of."

She looked at me like I had lost my damn mind. Then she stared at me, Cameron, Dollar then the house and back again.

"What are you doing here Ava?" she whispered. "They got you too?" she asked obviously traumatized in some kind of hoe twilight zone.

I looked back at Cameron who stood there with a blank expression plastered on his face. Dollar standing there with his big bully ass had his hands folded neatly in front of his body rocking back and forth on his snakeskin shoes. What grown as man teeters? He disgusted me.

It was time for me to take control I walked back to Cam's car shoulder bumping Dollar and grabbing my water. I stood in front of the two brothers and extended my palm telling one of them to give me the keys to their car. Dollar looked at me like I was insane. I may have been at that very moment but I was getting my friend out of there. I'd return once I took her to her parents so she could check on her father and got her somewhere comfortable. Cam gave his brother a look and shook his head.

I was most definitely was going to handle Dollar when I got back. He may have been the messiah to his hoes but that one he wasn't going to handle that way. If she chose to continue to do what she was doing all I could do was plant a seed it was up to her if she would allow it to grow. She was too pretty of a girl to be running around town selling her body to no good ass tricks. However, she was grown and I would be there for her. Cameron handed me his keys and I escorted a terrified Lauren to his car.

"See you soon," Dollar said waving and slapping Lauren on the ass causing her to jump as we passed him by. I kept it moving and told him to shut the hell up. I walked over to Cameron assuring him that I would be back in a few and drove Lauren to her parents' house.

On the way to their house Lauren told me about her father's cancer and how the events of the day transpired. She told me about working at the strip club and some hoes she got into it with in the dressing room her wife in laws whatever the hell that was and all of the people she had come in contact with working for Dollar. When she started talking about Chaz and Tamica her blood boiled and in the midst of all the craziness I had to laugh.

I swapped my own stories about my pregnancy and Cameron's crazy ass wife and of course the deranged cop who was after me and how moms put it down for me. It almost felt like old times but we were grown. I shook my head smiling the shit we'd gotten ourselves into. I confessed to wanting my boring life back.

When we got to her parents home the house was dark like no one was there. My stomach felt queasy the day was getting crazier by the minute I hoped that everything was ok. Although he spent a stint in prison for that murder Laurens dad was a good man. When he came back home from the penitentiary her life got better. I'd never say it directly to her but I couldn't stand her mother and the way she treated her. It was inevitable that if anything happened to Mr. Leslie Lauren and her mother would have it out.

We knocked on the door no one answered. Lauren pulled out her cell phone to call her mother. They were at the hospital. Panic stricken Lauren urged me to get in the car we needed to make our way to the other side of town. I didn't even get a chance to park good before Lauren was out the car running full speed into the building. I parked the car and casually strolled through the double doors. I walked past the reception area to the elevator and hit floor 8 for the oncology unit. I wanted to give Lauren some time with her parents alone. Not to mention I was not built for those types of things. I was way too emotional when it came to people I loved.

When I reached room 832 I stood just outside the doorway Lauren and her mother were engaged in a heated argument. Her mother was a piece of work. How could she even fix her lips to start an argument at a time like that? Lauren's father was suffering from cancer and Constance was standing in his hospital room calling his only child a black whore. Throwing pictures in her face of where she used the money that Lauren was abusing her body to get to pay their bills for a private investigator to show her father how much of a whore his daughter was.

That woman was out of her mind and all the mouth that Lauren had with everyone else she stood there and took the abuse from her mother. I wanted to run in there and come to her rescue but I couldn't that was a matter I couldn't concern myself with as bad as I wanted to and as much as I considered myself family I remained standing outside of the door until Lauren came storming out. She was so upset I don't even think she noticed me standing next to the door. Her father was calling out to her but he was so weak there was nothing he could do but hope she'd come back.

I couldn't take it anymore. I could remember her mother beating her ass when we were kids and she'd be running to our apartment in the middle of the night with her pajamas on crying because she had jumped on her. She didn't give her daughter the average beatings though. She gave her with what my granny called half killings. She'd literally be bloody. My mother took Lauren in quite a few times wanted to go over there and knock some sense into Constance her damn self but never did.

Maybe it was my hormones running unusually high because I was pregnant but her mother was going to know today exactly what it felt like to be slain with words. I had sharp tongue and I wasn't about to let up on Laurens so called mother. I walked into the room as Constance's eyes cut me like daggers. She never did like me but I didn't like her ass either so the feeling was mutual. I walked over to Mr. Leslie and placed a kiss on his forehead. He smiled saying, "How you doin' baby?"

Mr. Leslie was always like that as sweet as pie. I didn't understand how he had come to be with such an evil bitter ass bitch like Constance. I told him I was okay asked how he was feeling. He said he would be just fine it would take a lot more than cancer to put an OG down. I had to laugh. Even when the odds were placed against him he always managed to put others before himself. They didn't make men like him anymore.

We chopped it up a little more before I asked Constance if I could speak with her out in the hallway.

She reluctantly followed me because I didn't give her a chance to decline. I could tell by the strut and the look on her face that she thought she was going to come out in that hallway to check me too. But as my Uncle Nate would say wrong answer!

"And what can I help you with Ms. Ava?" she said with a smirk on her face crossing her arms.

"Well, Ms. Constance," I started. "First off I want to say you should be ashamed of yourself treating your daughter the way you do. At a time like this you should be creating as less stress as possible for Mr. Leslie and Lauren. She didn't ask to be here and she didn't ask for your pedophile brother to steal her innocence. You need to check yourself lady because when it's all said and done if you had ever been the mother you were supposed to be to her she wouldn't be in the position she is in today. You have no idea what that girl has been through and your attempts to taint and degrade her to make yourself feel better is a sign of weakness. You are a pathetic excuse for a mother. No I take that back you are pathetic excuse for a human being. I know all about you and if you were smart you'd straighten up before Lauren is not the only one trying to plead her case up in room 823."

When I was done I walked away not giving her a chance to say another word. The conversation was over. I didn't let her have it like I wanted to but I knew I had gotten my point across. Those days were over. Constance wasn't a saint. The entire time Mr. Leslie was locked up in prison she had many men running in and out of his bed. She was the biggest tramp in our neighborhood even had sex with one of Laurens boyfriends and she wanted to sit in there calling her daughter a whore.

I found Lauren sitting in the waiting room crying her eyes out. I asked her if she wanted to go home she said no she was going to stay at the hospital. I walked her into her father's room staring Constance down. At least she was quiet and didn't have any snide remarks falling from her mouth. I turned up my nose and bid Mr. Leslie and my best friend goodbye walking out the room with authority thinking at least something went in my favor today.

Although it was warm outside I got a sudden chill. I couldn't shake the feeling I had in the pit of my stomach. I dialed Cameron to let him know that I was on my way. He said he had some information for me but he didn't want to talk about it over the phone. I smiled he was turning hood on me. I attempted to crank up the car but it wouldn't turn over. How in the hell did Cameron have a shiny new Range Rover and it was acting a fool? I popped the hood to take a look. I didn't know what I was supposed to be looking for it sounded good though.

A well dressed elderly woman walked up to me asking if I needed any help. She was right on time I sure did. We tried to jump start the car but it still wouldn't start. I pulled out my cell phone to call Cameron I needed him to come get me. The woman insisted that she could take me where I needed to go. I told her I didn't want to cause her any trouble I was calling a ride. She asked where I was going. I gave her the general area. She said she was going that way anyway and could drop me off on the way.

I took a look at her license plate and texted Cam the number along with the make and model of the car just before my phone died. A woman could never be too careful these days and although something was telling me to go back inside the hospital and wait for the Powers boys to come get me I wanted to get out of that place as soon as possible. I sat in the woman's car strapping myself in the seat belt as we drove off.

The ride wasn't too long and I directed her all the way making small talk. She seemed like a pretty down to earth woman. When we got closer to Massachusetts Street I directed her to make a right but the woman kept going.

"You missed your turn," I said looking at her. All of a sudden the bitch got deaf. I started to get nervous. Why had I gotten in the car with this strange woman I didn't know shit about? I looked down at my phone sitting in my lap damn it was dead or else I could call Cameron. "Did you hear me? I said you missed your turn!" I said a little louder. Maybe she was really hard of hearing. She'd definitely heard me that time.

She reached to the radio and turned the music up. Oh hell no! I didn't know what the that bitch was on but I wasn't about to go through anymore drama she was going to let me out of that car and if she didn't she would regret she ever let me in that mothafucka. I reached to turn down the radio giving her one last chance to pull her ass over and let me out. I could walk the rest of the way to Dollars house.

"Listen lady today is not the day to be fucking with me!" I said my hand gripped firmly on the pistol that lay inside my purse. She didn't acknowledge a word I was saying as her phone began to ring.

"Yes, mhm okay yes I have her I am on my way," she said into the phone. I didn't know who she was talking to but she had the right idea but the wrong woman. I wasn't about to sit in that car waiting to find out where she was taking me or who she was taking me to. I had one up on her ass I had my pistol and was armed and dangerous. I didn't want to shoot her old ass but I would. No question about it.

I pulled my pistol out and spoke very calm and deliberate. "Let me out this damn car," I said cocking back the hammer and pressing the barrel to her temple. She dropped the phone into her lap and I could hear someone yelling asking what was going on. I snatched the phone up and pressed the speaker button.

"This old bitch can't come to phone right now," I said feeling myself. "Now tell her to pull the fuck over or she is one dead bitch." I said pressing on the trigger causing a bullet to whiz past the old woman's head and out the driver side window.

Obviously I was new to this gun shit because the woman jumped jerking the car sending us crashing into a tree on the side of the road. The airbags deployed knocking the gun out of my hand and knocking both of us senseless. I had on my seatbelt but it did nothing to help my cause other than to buy me a little time to escape.

My mind told me to get the hell out the car but my head was spinning too hard from the impact. I could feel blood trickling down my nose. The woman lay slumped over in her seat with a couple of bleeding scratches and scraps from the glass that had shattered. She was more out of it than I was. I felt around for my gun. I couldn't find it!

As I felt some of my strength coming back I noticed the old woman coming to. I needed to get the out the car. I fumbled around some more for the gun noticing it lying near her hand. My adrenaline started to kick in my mind was clicking a thousand miles per minute. I was only a couple blocks from Dollars house.

I went to reach for the gun as she came to swinging. She had a handful of my face clawing me as I tried to get a good grip on the gun. I could hear a police car in the distance I didn't want to be anywhere in sight when they got there. This whole situation was becoming bigger than the police I didn't know who I could trust until further notice.

I finally swept around and punched the woman dead in the middle of her face just as I gripped my pistol pulling the trigger simultaneously. I didn't know if I hit her or not didn't really care I heard her wail out in pain. I pressed the door open with all I had in me sprinting out the car and down the street to safety.

I could hear sirens in the distance. Damn I left my purse. I turned to go back to get it just as the woman started the car darting off into the darkness. Damn! I cursed to myself shit just got real she had all my shit! I made it to Dollars doorstep tired and out of breath as I banged for them to let me in. Cameron opened the door and I fell into his arms weeping.

"Come help me with her!" was all I heard him yell before I saw darkness.

# MARTEEN

## (18)

That bitch must have had nine lives or something. She kept slipping through my fingers. I was tired of playing nice with her. I'd looked through daddy's files in his office and found Sophia's number. She'd been in the business for many years. I'd seen her in my home on several different occasions being paid for her superb services. Ask me she was overrated being that she'd failed at bringing me a simple ass ghetto bitch within two hours. If I ever needed those types of services again I'd opt to call Miguel.

Ms. Delores was in the guest bedroom sleeping. I had brought her home, cleaned her up and called Perry over to take a look at her wound. It was just a flesh wound the bullet had barely grazed her. He'd given her a pain pill and told me to keep her in the bed.

Perry and I'd had a little fling many years ago when Cameron and I first got married. He was good at keeping secrets. He had given me a shot when I came down with an STD from cheating on my husband. I'd slept with him after the antibiotic ran its' course to show my thanks. I had given him the pussy he needed when his wife didn't want to fuck. We were good for each other. No one ever overstepped their boundaries and our relationship was strictly business.

Chester sat on my couch pouting as Perry and I made small talk before he left. I didn't know what he was so hot under the collar for. I ignored him as I normally did and continued with my flirting until Perry left for the hospital. He was a decent man but I didn't dare tell him all of my business a woman could never be too careful with the skeletons in her closet.

I'd told Perry my mother was in an accident and didn't want to go to the hospital and I couldn't get in contact with Cameron. He rushed over like he normally did when I told him I needed him and took care of Ms. Delores right away. When Perry left the house it was mandatory that I address Chester.

He had been so rude. Acting like he was the king of my castle. He was a guest in my home and he'd better get that straight. Before I could say a word Yasmine came running into the room to show me a picture she'd colored. I didn't have time to look. There were things that needed to be taken care of.

"Mommy, mommy," she smiled running into the room tugging on my pant leg. If no one would have been in the room I would have kicked her and sent her on her way. Why did I have a child? I often questioned myself. I hated children.

I shot her look causing her to lower her head and walk out of the room. Why couldn't she just be quiet most of the time? I didn't feel like hearing the giggling and laughing the whining it wore my patience thin. Children were to be seen and not heard. I should have left her with my parents even though they told me they'd had plans for the next two weeks. The Caribbean was calling their names. What were grandparents for if they were always gone? Go figure they weren't much of parents either.

I sat down with Chester as we mapped out our next move. I wanted Ava dead. I had way too much to lose if I let her live mainly my husband. I was going back and forth with sparing his life. She had taken him from me. She'd probably been fucking around with him long before I'd found out which pissed me off even more. If Cameron wanted to stand in the way and be her savior he could go to hell right along with her.

He was going to have to choose me or her.

"Marteen," Chester said interrupting the thoughts I was having of my husband being with another woman.

"What?" I snapped staring at him in disgust.

"What is the real reason you are after this woman?" he asked.

Oh now all of a sudden he wanted to have a conscious a fucking eureka moment when it all came together and he realized I was using his ass he'd be hurt. So fucking what! Tough! He allowed himself to be used. I didn't know why he was questioning me when unfortunately for him there wasn't any turning back now. He had to finish what he started rather he liked the reasoning behind it or not.

"Does it really matter Chester?" I asked not hiding that I was annoyed by his questioning.

"As a matter of fact it does!" he shot back matching my tone. Chester had never talked to me in that manner he always did whatever I told him to do. If he didn't shut his mouth he would be going to meet his maker a little sooner than I had anticipated and a lot sooner than he was aware of.

"You," I said pointing in his face. "Are treading on very thin ice." I countered back. "If you would've done the job right in the first place I wouldn't have to run around trying to clean up this mess." I was going to continue but I cut my verbal assault short. "You know what just shut your dumb ass up and let me do the talking." I told him going back into strategy mode.

He remained silent staring me down. At that point I wished I was a mind reader so I could curse him out for every thought he was having in that little bitty brain of his.

"I'm a man!" he shouted out of nowhere.

"No shit," I feigned ignorance to his statement.

Chester jumped off the couch and begin pacing the floor and running his hands over his head. He was losing his cool.

"Sit down," I demanded. "Calm down okay," I directed in a more smooth tone. I didn't feel like the dramatics at the moment and time was of the essence. I asked him to sit tight as I went to the kitchen to retrieve drinks to put him at ease for a while. I mixed a little elixir my mother had concocted into his drink. It paid to have a mother who was a Mambo.

I made sure to carry his drink in my right hand. When I re entered the room Chester was still pacing. I urged him to sit down relax and share a drink with me handing him the liquid. He gulped it down and sat the glass on the table. Shaking my head to keep from going off about how uncouth he was I sipped my drink as I ran down the game plan.

I hated Ava with every ounce of hate in my body. My bones hurt from hating her so much. I even hated to say her name. Once I got my hands on her I would do things to her she couldn't imagine even in her worst nightmare. She had ruined my life with her whorish ways.

After I'd etched the plan into Chester's head four times I sat back and enjoyed the smoothness of the cognac that was traveling down my throat. I could feel my own eyes getting low as the alcohol warmed my body. I smiled at Chester he was always more tolerable when I was under the influence.

He gave me a fake ass smile and turned his head away. Something was up with him and I wasn't feeling it at all. I had caught him a couple times whispering on the phone to someone. Or he'd excuse himself to take a phone call or two. To be honest his phone rang too damn much he'd better not have another woman he was seeing. Chester had been mine since high school. Even during Lorenzo I dated Chester.

"What's wrong?" I asked him as I stood behind him on the sofa massaging his massive shoulders. He was hesitant to speak. I waited for what seemed like forever before he opened his mouth.

"Do you love me like I love you Marteen?" here he had to ruin the moment with his sentimental bullshit. Of course I didn't love him the way he loved me. Why did he think a man like him could be with a woman like me? It didn't take a rocket scientist to see that we weren't compatible.

"Of course I love you," I lied continuing to massage him deeper.

"Then why are you after your husband's girlfriend? Why can't we just be together?" he asked sounding like a little boy speaking to his mother.

I stopped my massage. He had officially blown my high. He wasn't as dumb as I thought he was but that didn't matter. It was water under the bridge. I sat in a chair to facing him.

"We are together," pretending to be clueless to what he was getting at and avoiding the question about Ava. "Contrary to what you might believe she is not his girlfriend." I said trying to convince him he had it all wrong.

"I'm going to lose my job because of you, may even go to jail if his girlfriend runs to the police and they investigate." He said looking pitiful. He was telling me like I gave a damn about him losing his job or going to jail. He was folding under pressure right before my very eyes. I couldn't have that not then not ever.

"Listen," I said snapping by fingers to get his attention and maneuvering myself into his face. "She's not going to tell anybody anything. Dead women don't talk." I said seriously. "You trust me right?" I asked pushing his chin upward making him look me in the eyes. He needed a pep talk and I was just the one to give it to him. He shook his head yes. "So get your head into the game boy! Your football career ain't got shit on the games we are about to play. I'm playing for keeps." I said as a smile crept across my face.

His faith in me hadn't deteriorated he nodded his head smiling and pulling me into him giving me a hard sloppy kiss. Things were about to get real. The elixir was working it helped calm him down and put him on my level. It was almost time to get down to business.

I excused myself so I could go upstairs to change clothes. I heard whispering in my daughter's room. I stood at the door listening but I couldn't quite make out what was being said. I burst into the room. "Who are you talking to?" I said snatching the phone from her hands.

"Hello?" I said. There was no answer I looked at the caller id it was her father. Why did he have to teach her how to use a cell phone she was only three years old? *Just in case of an emergency Yasmine that says D A D dad just hit this and I will answer whenever you call.* That's the bullshit he told her.

I stared at Yasmine her eyes big as saucers. Although I knew who she was talking to I wanted to hear her tell me.

"Did you hear me?" I asked kneeling down getting up close and personal our noses almost touching. She stood there staring at me with those big gray eyes. It was midnight and she was sneaking on a phone in my house.

I snatched her up by her hair overwhelmed with rage. "Who were you talking to little girl?" I demanded slinging her onto the bed by her hair. She let out a yelp and cried out for her daddy.

That just fueled my fire even more. I began to hit that little girl. Before I knew it I was being dragged away and Ms. Delores was in the room hovered over Yasmine the way she used to comfort me when mama would get mad about daddy being gone all the time.

I stared at them both in disdain. Again Yasmine had taken someone from me. She took my parents; she took Cameron, and now Ms. Delores. I screamed for Chester to let me go but he had a good grip on me. I hated that little girl I gave birth to.

"What did you tell him?" I screamed as Chester man handled me all the way down the stairs. Hearing the piercing screams of Yas reminded me of the memories I had in my own childhood. Memories I'd wanted to bury for such a long time. Mommy loved that damn dog more than she loved me that's why I set it on fire.

Fire! In that instance I was taken back to those red flames the smell of burning hair and flesh. I was only nine years old but the image was still embedded in my head forever. That was when I became obsessed with watching things die. I'd tie cats' tails together then watch them tear each other apart. I could see my victim's very soul leaving their eyes and then nothing.

I imagined myself stealing their souls and becoming a super human. I couldn't be stopped I wouldn't be stopped because I had the power to give and take away. I was a goddess. I eluded power with just my presence. I could be the angel of death or a lifeline. It was me Marteen LeBlanc that held the future of the world in her hands.

"Marteen!" Chester barked pulling me out of my rage. "What the hell is wrong with you?" he pleaded.

"She told him Chester," I said. "Do you want to go to jail? Do you want to lose your job?" I asked. I didn't know what she had said but I needed him on my side. I needed him to help me get rid of Yasmine, Cameron, and Ava. I didn't have enough time to plan and plot by myself he was the muscle I was the brains.

Panic stricken he answered, "No!"

Picking up the kitchen knife I handed it to him. "Well then you know what to do," I said looking upstairs towards Yasmine's room.

I waited as Chester stalked his way up the stairs to rid myself of one less person to give me grief. I listened intently waiting for the screams that never came. Chester appeared at the top of the stairs with a look of bewilderment on his face.

"What are you waiting for?" I screamed irritated shaking my head furiously.

"They're gone!" he said.

"What do you mean they are gone?" I questioned taking two stairs at a time to reach the top.

"No one's in here see," he said following behind me as I searched Yasmine's room for her and Ms. Delores.

"You look downstairs and I will look up here," I said in a low tone. "They couldn't have gotten too far," I said instructing Chester to head downstairs to find them.

"They got out! They got out!" Chester yelled from downstairs in a panic. I came rushing down the stairs to see the kitchen door leading to the garage wide open.

"Fuck!" I cursed going to get my keys from the key holder in the kitchen near the garage. The second I noticed they were gone I heard a loud crash and screeching tires. Ms. Delores and Yas were in the car heading down the driveway burning rubber down the road.

Chester and I in sync jumped in my Jaguar ready to track them down. My cell phone started to ring I looked down not noticing the number. I hit ignore and continued to drive. The number kept calling over and over. I couldn't answer it I was too busy searching for any sign of my car.

"They're going to the police! I know it!" Chester screamed as he hit the dashboard.

"Shut up!" I demanded trying to think. My mind was racing I didn't know what to do. I was thinking maybe I could just skip town and lay low for a little while. I couldn't run my entire life. My thoughts were running altogether. All of a sudden I wasn't feeling so confident I had a headache.

"What we gone do Marteen?" Chester asked looking to me for answers. I didn't know what the hell he was going to do but I wasn't going down. He would go down all by himself. I could convince everyone that he made me do it. No one would believe that I was capable of such things. He was the crazy one.

He had attacked Ava not me. No one had even seen me except Ms. Delores she was just emotional at the time she wouldn't dare tell on me. Not after what she did so many years ago. It was him that had been following Ava and stalking her, it was him that had been stalking me I had hundreds of text messages from him many of which I didn't respond to and many with me telling him to leave me alone. I never responded to his texts unless I didn't want to be bothered and if I did want to be bothered I would call him from the prepaid phone that I had purchased.

I couldn't go to prison or a mental institution. Daddy would get me out. He didn't have a choice I was his daughter his only child he wouldn't dare turn his back on me. If he tried I would tell how he covered up what happened to Alexis but then they would know my secret. The voices in my head were screaming.

Chester wasn't the only one panicking I was losing it too. I didn't know what to do. Where were they? I needed to find my car before it was too late.

# LAUREN

## (19)

My dad had convinced me into going home to get some rest promising me that he was alright. I had never experienced so many emotionally draining situations in less than 24 hours in my life. My mother didn't make the shit at the hospital any more comfortable but I was glad she'd kept her mouth shut.

I didn't want to be alone. I needed someone to keep me company. I wasn't calling Dollar. Not after the way he had treated me. After all I'd done for him and with him. We were through. He could've come with me to check on my dad but instead he was on some I'm a pimp shit. I was questioning everything and everyone who had a position in my life.

Going through the motions I started naming off those who were expendable and those who were not. I could call Brooke I thought but she had to work she was always working. She was into the nightlife just like me but she loved Molly. Me on the other hand I was just high off the life period.

Chaz! I thought. He was probably laid up somewhere with Tamica's hoe ass. Who was I to call Tamica a hoe? She wasn't a hoe that bitch was a mud duck, a skeezer, a hood rat, one of them ratchet bitches she wasn't getting money from none of the niggas she gapped her legs open for. I strolled outside the hospital pulling a pack of Newport's from my purse.

I looked over at the no smoking sign and rolled my eyes. I was lighting a cigarette right in front of that damn door and I dared somebody to say something to me. I was mad I didn't have any weed or else I'd be high as kite by my damn self at about that time. Smoke my ass into oblivion and get a good nights' rest.

I called a cab to come pick me up and take me over to the hood. Hell even if Chaz had somebody over there I needed to get my shit. They had too many niggas running in and out of there and I needed the money I took from Dollar. I laughed to myself I had become a bitch with no fear damn near overnight.

When I got to the spot things were pretty quiet for a Saturday night. The usual crowd was hanging around outside but it wasn't crackin' like it would have normally been. Then again I hadn't been to the neighborhood at that time of the morning in a long time so maybe that had become the norm.

I paid the cab driver and walked up the stairs to the apartment. I could hear the music pumping loudly through the speakers. It was a party going on inside go figure there was always a party going on over there. People ran in and out of that apartment nonstop. Business was always conducted out of that building twenty four hours a day. No one actually lived there but there was always someone guarding what was inside.

No one ever called the police because no outsiders were welcome in the small community. The junkies were happy and the children enjoyed the couple dollars they got for running errands for the drug dealers who owned the place.

They didn't have violence in the neighborhood other than the small beefs that ended in a fist fight. Chaz and Marcus ran the projects with an iron fist no one broke the rules unless they had a death wish.

I'd seen Chaz angry before and it wasn't anything I'd choose to see again. He was a caring man to those he loved but he could be a beast in the streets. He didn't take anything lightly and when it came to loyalty he spared no one when they crossed the line. He had a zero tolerance policy. Anyone could be terminated for misconduct.

I understood his logic he had to carry himself that way. People from these parts tended to take kindness for weakness especially when you ran a drug empire. Most people were unaware of just how much Chaz was worth because he dressed in khakis, a crisp white t-shirt, a clean pair of kicks, and a different hat every day. However, the trained eye would notice the Rolex that dangled from his wrist and know he was definitely holding something.

I walked up to the door turning the knob and entering into another thick cloud of smoke. The house was jammed packed with people standing, talking, drinking and smoking. That was their way of life. Everyone lived for the moment some with regrets others never had a care in the world. I squeezed my way through the crowd shoving a bitch that saw me trying to get through but decided not to move out of my way. I made a mental note to check her ass before I left.

I entered the kitchen searching the room of what seemed like a hundred faces. The smoke was burning my eyes and I was catching a much needed contact. I wasn't complaining my day had been hell if I wasn't on a mission I'd be rolling up myself. I spotted Marcus; Chaz's younger brother leaned up against a wall in the corner. He sported a permanent scold on his face as he surveyed two men on the other side of the room.

I greeted Marcus with a hug and a peck on the cheek.

"What's going on baby bruh?" I asked shoulder bumping him. He shook his head never taking his eyes off the men. I knew that look and immediately was ready to get on. I didn't have time to deal with anymore drama and for sure wasn't about to be in the middle of the kind of drama that Marcus was about to be on. "Where's Chaz?" I yelled into his ear. Still staring the men down he pointed his finger in the air. That was my queue to head upstairs get my stuff and exit stage left or right it didn't matter just as long as I got out of there before whatever was about to go down went down.

I sauntered my way back through the multitude of people towards the stairs in pursuit of getting my things. I stepped to Roc and Monsta who were standing at the bottom making sure no one unauthorized made their way up. They let me through and I strolled one step at a time to my destination.

My intentions had been to throw a little bit of shade at Chaz for having Tamica at the house earlier. He could have done way better than that and he didn't have to be all up on her in my face either. We weren't together would never be together because he had too many bitches he dealt with but the least he could have done was respected me and put on his little show out of my presence.

I rolled my eyes in my head just thinking about him and her all hugged up in the kitchen. Upstairs was fairly quiet there weren't any people filling the halls or the bedrooms. I could hear voices coming from the room on the far right. I crept up to the door not knowing what I would run into.

As I got closer I realized it hadn't been a conversation I was walking up on. Those were moans. I peeked through the cracked door and my eyes widened as I watched Chaz beating Tamica from behind while she ate another female. He was pulling out and slamming hard back into her with a vengeance. I was mad and damn sure jealous but I couldn't stop watching them. My adrenaline started pumping I wanted to fight and fuck all at the same time.

I started comparing myself to her. In my mind she wasn't hotter than me. Her ass wasn't fatter than mine, her features weren't as pretty as mines, she didn't know how to get money, had nothing going for herself but being the ratchet ass bitch she was. I couldn't take it anymore my blood was boiling. I didn't care that he wasn't my man I wanted to cuss him and her the fuck out. All these years he wanted me nothing changed. He was just all hugged up with me a few months ago.

I didn't give him the time of day because he wasn't serious. He'd had the nerve to throw that rat up in my face like that? I busted through the door causing everybody to jump and turn their attention to me. I twisted my face like I smelled something that stank. I actually did smell something that stank one of them nasty hoes must have had some bacterial vaginosis going on because they snatch smelled like straight fish.

"I just came to get my shit," I said with an attitude leaving them all looking at me like I was crazy. Walking past everyone I began snatching up my bags. I looked at Chaz and told him he needed to put some damn clothes on and help me take my stuff out to the cab I was about to call. He was still on his knees behind Tamica looking at me with a smirk on his face. The girl lying underneath Chaz's nasty new girlfriend was fiddling with the sheets to cover her body.

"Oh don't flatter yourself sweetheart," I said tilting my head to the side and staring at her. "You ain't got shit I want to see."I said smacking my lips and calling another cab. I didn't know why I had made the driver I'd rode over there with leave in the first place.

Of course Ms. Tamica decided she wanted to fix her lips and attempt to say something but she was cut off immediately. "And you don't need to say shit either," I said rolling my neck and pointing my finger at her. I wanted a reason to go upside her head. I couldn't stand the bitch.

She looked at Chaz as if he was going to say something. "I don't know what you looking at him for he ain't gon' do shit," I said looking between him and her like I wish you mothafuckas would. He stood there laughing like I was some kind of joke it only pissed me off more.

"Come here," he said pulling my arm to get me closer to him. I wasn't sure if he was crazy or just plain stupid. Why in the hell would he pull me to him and he was still knee deep in that nasty bitch birth canal. Nigga please.

"Quit playing nigga you need to help me since you done knocked all this shit out my damn bag," I grumbled slapping his hand away and throwing his boxers in his face. "Put your damn clothes on and help me put my shit in the car." The scene was unreal everybody was still in the same position as when I busted in looking at me as I went on my little tirade mumbling and talking shit as I slammed the things that had fallen out of bag back inside.

Chaz thought it was amusing, Tamica looked at me with what looked like lust in her eyes, and the anonymous random chicken head just looked plain embarrassed. She may have been the only one of the trio who had a little bit of sense. I shook my head in disgust and told him to hurry up with the rest of my stuff while I dragged my bags out the door and down the stairs to wait for my ride.

I wasn't even sure where I was going to go. My house was off limits Dollar knew where I lived and I wanted to rest. Daddy had sent me away from the hospital. I was driving myself crazy worrying about him. He was my father I couldn't help it I hated to see him in so much pain and there was nothing I could do about it. My mother had been acting a fool having someone follow me because she so called knew I was up to no good. Told me I was a whore then and I was a whore now. She had been testing me a lot. Truth was I felt like if she didn't tighten up soon things would get physically ugly for her. The days of her abuse were over if she needed the memo I could definitely give it to her.

Then Ava and Dollars brother! What the hell kind of shit was she on? I thought she was dating some big time doctor from her job? She had fallen off again dating another street nigga. When all this shit died down I was going to have a talk with my friend. She was much better than that she didn't have to settle for less she really had her shit together. It was me that couldn't seem to get it quite right.

I stood outside with my trash bags full of clothing waiting on the curb for a cab. Ten minutes later Chaz strolled out the door with the remainder of my clothes and shoes. He stood next to me staring. I pretended like he wasn't staring as I looked straight ahead. He laughed to himself which burned my ass but I still didn't say anything. I wasn't about to feed into his little antics.

"What you so mad for?" he asked poking me in my side. I wasn't entertaining him with an answer. He knew why I was mad but I wasn't playing those games. I was in the driver seat never the passenger.

"Mad?" I said twisting my face for the umpteenth time that day. "Get over yourself sweetheart. Do you."

He stared at me like he was confused. He opened his mouth like he was about to say something but opted to keep it shut because the look on my face said don't even go there. There was really nothing to talk about. He could do whatever he wanted to do. He just needed to stop flirting with me and telling me how good we would be together every time we were around each other.

Sure I dealt with other men and put him off when he approached me. If he really felt like that though he would have tried harder but he didn't, he'd just move on to the next bitch. When I said no he was supposed to make me a believer. He should have pulled out all the stops for me because I was that bitch there wasn't another bitch on the earth like me. Tamica wasn't me.

My ride pulled up and before it had come to a complete stop I was opening the door throwing bags into the backseat. I instructed the driver to pop the trunk so we could load the rest of my life inside. Damn I thought to myself what was I becoming? I reached inside a bag digging in the spot that I'd tucked the money I'd stolen and smiled as my fingers ran across the thick wads of bills. I quickly stuffed all of it in my handbag.

I strutted to the other side of the cab and pulled the door open to hop in.

"Lauren," Chaz called out to me in the most sincere voice I'd heard all night. I looked back at him just as gunshots rang out in the house followed by screams as people rushed out the front door falling down the steps getting trampled.

Chaz signaled for me to leave as he turned running back towards the house in a frenzy. I knew some shit was about to jump off I just didn't know there would be gunplay involved. I hopped inside the cab and urged the driver to drive off. His mama couldn't have raised no fool because Habib burnt rubber up outta there hitting the curb as we bent the corner all gas no breaks. I looked back at all the mayhem as I said a silent prayer for Chaz.

I didn't know what was going on but I felt in my gut that it wasn't all good. Marcus was always on edge but the look in his eyes I'd noticed was one I'd never seen before. His eyes were cold and calculated he meant business. I reached for my cell phone and dialed Ava's number. No one picked up.

I wasn't feeling that considering the last I knew she was going to be in the presence of a psychotic ass pimp and his brother who couldn't have been any less psychotic than he. I contemplated calling Dollar and demanding to speak to my best friend instead I called Brooke which was who I should have called in the first damn place. It was her brothers that were having a shoot out with what I assumed were some off brand ass niggas.

"Hello?" Brooke yelled into the receiver clearly wide awake at the wee hours of the morning still going strong.

"I can't talk on the phone right now but it's about Chaz and Marcus I need you to meet me at my house." I said.

"My brothers can take care of themselves Lauren I'm busy," she said with an attitude. I didn't know what the fuck was going on with this little bitch but her tongue had gotten a whole lot more slick lately and I wasn't feeling that shit. I know she thought she was billy bad ass but she wasn't going to talk to me crazy.

"Yeah yeah yeah I understand all that but I need to holla at you but not on the phone. I'll see you in a minute," I said hanging up before she could say anything. I didn't know if she was going to bring her little ass to the house or not but I tried. She must have been laid up with Cebo's crazy ass. He had that girls mind gone and probably some mo' shit.

## CAMERON

## (20)

We drove to the hospital full speed with me in a panic. I was a medical doctor and didn't know what the hell to do with myself. I could help hundreds of people make them feel better but when Ava passed out at that front door and I saw blood flowing from between her legs my mind literally went blank. My brother had to call 911 and I just stood there in shock.

It never should have gotten this far. I should have left Marteen alone a long time ago and never looked back. Cut off all communication. I loved my daughter but it was obvious I couldn't deal with a psychotic and delusional woman without the court system involved. I would have to just do things the right way. I didn't have time to deal with the all the drama. Now the mother of my second child was threatening to miscarry all because I wanted to bow down to a crazy ass woman.

All the signs and I ignored them. I chose to sit around playing her games on her terms never putting my foot down always being the fool. I'd never been the victim of any woman. Why had I started with Marteen? I put my head in my hands shaking from side to side. My head hurt I couldn't think straight. I could feel my brother staring at me as he drove behind the ambulance.

He played hard but Dollar had a heart too. I don't know how he ended up the way he did but he loved hard especially his little brother. I knew he was worried if not for Ava for me because I was worried for Ava. She was battered, worn and pregnant all because of me. I felt guilty and I felt like wringing Marteens' neck.

It was funny how one could be head over heels in love with someone one day and want to choke the life out of them the next. She had taken me there. She didn't know Ava was pregnant but I knew if she did that things would have been a lot worse. That bitch didn't have any compassion she was as heartless as cold steel. If I saw her at that very moment I was catching a case and that was on everything I loved.

"Aye, man she gon' be aight," Dollar said glancing over at me.

That was something I knew but I felt guilty. I couldn't control Marteen and I knew she had to be behind everything that was happening to Ava up until this point. Now she was riding in an ambulance miscarrying our baby. I knew Marteen was a lot of things but it never crossed my mind she would go to the extreme of trying to physically harm someone. Her family had a violent past. I didn't want to cross her father but when it came to those that I loved I guess I'd have to take my chances.

I wasn't like my brother I wasn't the type of man to put my hands on a woman but my hands were tied. I had to go hard for her to understand that this shit wasn't a game. Lives were at stake and my patience was gone. I didn't want to go to war with the LeBlanc Family. Win, lose or draw it was about to go down because Jean LeBlanc didn't put his foot down when it came to his psychotic ass daughter.

She had mental problems. The woman needed some serious help. Regardless of what she was going through as soon as I made sure Ava was alright I was going to get my daughter and there wasn't a damn thing she would be able to do about it unless I wasn't breathing. Marteen had become a live wire and I personally felt as if no one was safe around her. Not even her own child.

When my daughter called to tell me that she'd over heard her mother and some man talking about killing Ava I should have been shocked but I wasn't. The longer I knew this woman the more I saw how unstable she truly was. I'd told Yasmine to calm down and promised her daddy would be there to get her soon. Then the phone went dead.

I'd tried to call back on several different occasions but the phone kept going to voicemail. My gut was telling me something wasn't quite right. In the midst of the turmoil I was feeling I tried to reason with myself that she wouldn't do anything to hurt her own child but I wasn't so sure. As I sat in the passenger seat going back and forth in my head I had this overwhelming feeling that I needed to go see about my daughter.

I pulled out my cell and called up to the hospital asking to speak with Ms. Pam. She was one of the only employees I trusted whole heartedly. She was a mother figure to most of us who worked there. I told her that Ava was on her way to the ER threatening a miscarriage and whatever she did don't let any visitors in the room I didn't care who they claimed to be.

Of course she had a lot of questions but I had to cut the conversation short telling her I would explain later to just do as I asked and I believed that Ava was in danger. Ms. Pam was spooked. She didn't like the sound of that and said she would be calling the police immediately. I told her I would be there as soon as I could I needed to handle something and would talk to her when I got there.

"Doctor Powers you be careful," she said with concern in her voice.

I assured her that I would be fine and disconnected the call. Looking at Dollar I told him to head back to the home that Marteen and I once shared. He looked at me like I was crazy.

"Listen man," I said speaking in an even tone. "I have to get my daughter up out of that house. I don't know what that woman is capable of."

Dollar let out a long sigh and made a u-turn in the middle of the street. "Dollar told you about that bitch lil' bruh," he said clearly irritated with all the drama I was having. "That bitch is evil always has been it's in her eyes. They're empty," he said seriously. "We get my niece and get the hell on because you might not be the type of nigga to lay a bitch out but I will choke that bitch unconscious." He said not cracking a smile.

I hated putting my brother in the middle of my bullshit but I didn't have anyone else to turn to. Mama could have tried to go get Yasmine for me but after their last run in I didn't want mama anywhere near Marteen she might have laid her out as well.

I never thought I'd deal with a woman who disrespected my mama. When the shit went down I was tempted myself to go upside her head but of course Marteen put on a show twisting the truth to make it seem as if my mama was in the wrong. Playing the victim card with me as she usually did making me want to be her protector.

Sitting there I shook my head in disgust. Everyone had told me about Marteen but her fat ass, light skin, pretty hair, and exotic eyes wouldn't let me see into her soul. I was stunned by her beauty. Her beauty didn't get me anywhere but sitting in a car with my brother stressed the fuck out.

My thoughts were interrupted with Dollar questioning what the fuck had happened at my old home. I looked up and blinked twice to make sure my eyes weren't playing tricks on me. The front door was left wide open it looked like every light in the house was on and the garage door was busted through with debris filling the driveway. As I looked at the scene in front of me my stomach began to turn. I felt like I had to use the bathroom there was a lump caught in my throat.

Dollar turned off the lights and the engine of the car and signaled for me to be quiet. He didn't have to tell me twice I didn't know what was going on inside the house but I knew one thing for damn sure my baby girl had better been alright or Mr. Powers would be going to be on a rampage something serious and nobody would be safe.

We crept up to the front door of the house making sure we didn't touch anything. We didn't want to disturb anything just in case the police needed to be there. I should have called them but knowing Marteen it was possible she could have been having one of her temper tantrums and fucked up the house just on G.P. she was silly like that.

We tiptoed through the house slipping into every room Dollar with his pistol in hand and me ready to throw hands about mine. The house was empty we stood in the middle of the living room stumped. I didn't know what in the hell was going on but I wasn't feeling right. We stared at each other not saying a word both of our minds clicking a hundred miles an hour trying to make sense of the scene before us.

As we exited the house I noticed something in the bushes. I took a look closer and it was a shoe. I grabbed Dollars arm whispering for him to take a look. The shoe was so tiny I thought recognizing the pink boots I had purchased for Yasmine only a few weeks earlier. My stomach began to do somersaults as I tried to catch my breath.

I was thinking the worst. I wasn't a man who cried often but the emotional rollercoaster I was riding was causing me to break down. I was filled with sadness and anger didn't know which I felt the most. The rage that was building inside me made me feel as if I was about to burst into a walking a flame torching any and every living organism in sight.

Everything around me started to spin. I started to become unraveled as I looked at my daughter. Stuck and blinded by fear I couldn't stand it. There could be only one reason why she was alone in those bushes. I couldn't take it. Dollar took control of the situation snatching Yasmine up causing her to yelp out in the fear.

That was the sweetest sound I had ever heard in my life. My adrenaline was still pumping my breathing still erratic but my baby girl was alright. My body still wouldn't allow me to move as I watched my little girl scream out her uncle's name and hold on to his neck for dear life weeping as her body trembled.

I had never saw my brother shed a tear in my life but at that very moment I watched as he held his niece in his arms rocking and consoling her he shed many tears. She hadn't even noticed me standing there. I'd never saw my daughter so fearful before. I would find out exactly what happened but for the time being I had to get her to safety.

We ran back to Dollars beat up Cadillac. As soon as Yaz noticed me sitting in the backseat waiting for her she screamed daddy and jumped into my arms. I held her tight never wanting to let her go. She was hysterical and although she was only three years old she told me a story I never wanted to hear again.

Guilt began to fill me once again. I knew better than to leave her in the care of Marteen but I had left her there anyway just to keep the peace with an insane woman. You couldn't compromise or reason with someone whose mind was gone. There would be no more compromising on my behalf. If Marteen thought she was getting within 50 feet of my daughter I would drop her where she stood. If anybody had anything to say about it I'd lay their ass down as well.

Cameron the medical professional was gone. I was a madman and somebody was going to pay for my daughter's pain. I looked at her with pain in my eyes. There was a large red handprint on the side of her face from her mother slapping her. Her hair was a mess. There was bruising all over her small frame.

Neither Dollar nor I said a word as we drove in silence to take her to the hospital. I hadn't been to sleep in over twenty four hours. I wouldn't be sleeping for however long it took to find my soon to be ex-wife and the man she'd gotten to partake in the assault of my daughter. It was on and I was taking no prisoners and sparing no one. Marteen had no idea of the man I'd used to be.

I pulled up to the hospital rushing my daughter inside. They got Yasmine back to a room immediately. We were later greeted by the authorities. I allowed my daughter to give them the gruesome details of all she had experienced living with her mother. It hurt me that she had been too afraid to tell me all that had been going on. I was amazed at how her three year old mind could recollect so much and verbalize to them in great detail.

She told them of a man who drove a police car and wore a uniform. The two detectives in plain clothing gave each other a knowing look and nodded to one another. My mind began to wander back to Ava and the police officer who had been stalking her. As she described him I began to picture the man following Ava the day we'd ran into each other at the ice cream parlor. I knew exactly who he was I never forgot a face.

When the detectives walked into the hallway I followed them promising Yasmine daddy would be right back. She cried for me not to leave her. I directed Ms. Pam to come inside the room to care for her until I finished talking to the detectives. I could tell by their demeanor they had something they wanted to tell me. I urged them to tell me what they were going to do but they informed me that it was an ongoing investigation they couldn't tell me anything just yet.

Marteen would have a warrant out for her arrest for child endangerment, child neglect, child abuse, and some more shit. All the while I was thinking they'd better get to her before I did or she would be a dead bitch. I pretended to empathize with them signaling for my brother to follow them. Dollar was on it he stayed ready. And as much as he disrespected and mistreated other people's daughters, mothers, sisters, nieces and the like he wasn't feeling anyone disrespecting the women he loved.

I shook the detective's hands and headed to the room they had Ava in. She lay in the bed hooked up to an I.V. she was dehydrated and sleeping peacefully courtesy of the pain medication that was given to her. Sitting next to her bed I grabbed her hand kissing it softly apologizing to her for everything she had been through. Both of my leading ladies were in hospital beds.

Ava opened her eyes a little bit and let her mouth curl into a weak smile. Even through all the bullshit she was still smiling. They said the baby would be okay she just needed to take it easy and stop stressing. I intended on making sure she did just that. I was taking some leave to get my life in order.

She tried to sit up but I motioned for her to just relax. "I'm okay," she said weakly.

"I know you're okay," I responded. "You still need your rest you've had a long night." I said. She'd been assaulted, kidnapped, and in a car accident in addition to being chased down by my brother the infamous pimp named Dollar all within 24 hours. She was going through hell. I didn't need her going through anymore so I opted not to say anything about Yasmine.

"You ain't never lied," she chuckled. I didn't know how the hell she found any humor in what was going on but that was exactly what I admired about her. She was optimistic even when the odds were placed against her. "I still have you though," she smiled looking me in the eyes.

We talked for a few more minutes then I told her I had to make a couple runs. She looked disappointed but didn't say anything. I wanted to tell her exactly what was going on but I didn't need her to worry anymore than she already was. I told her I was recommending that they keep her for at least another twenty fours for observation.

She tried to say she was okay but I wasn't taking no for an answer. That was more than enough time for either me or the police to get to Marteen. I kissed her on the forehead then the lips and started to exit.

"Take Yas to my mama's house she will be safe over there," she called after me.

I turned to look at her. How the hell did she know what had happened to Yas? "Dollar," was all she said. My brother must have really taken to Ava he didn't talk to women for shit unless he was trying to mack them down. He for damn sure wasn't going to check on them in a hospital room. I smiled and nodded in agreement. My daughter would be safe with Ms. Tanner and the rest of the kids.

## MARTEEN

## (21)

Things always worked out in my favor I was standing there in front of Delores who was tied and beaten in the basement of my fathers' home. They were out of town on another vacation. I had access to their home any time I pleased and I was glad I didn't have to go through answering twenty one questions. The LeBlanc home was situated on fifteen acres in the middle of nowhere.

No one would hear her scream. The old bitch hadn't gotten to the police station fast enough. We spotted her crashed into my car and snatched her ass up. I was pissed when she didn't have Yasmine in the car with her. And the bitch had more heart than she did when I was teenager because she wasn't giving her up either.

Yasmine was only three years old. I knew Delores didn't leave her out in the open so that someone could find her. Weren't too many places that she could have taken her. To those old boarded up houses I'd bet. After we had gotten her tied up in the basement I sent Chester to go get Yas and bring her back.

It wouldn't be hard to get rid of both of them. We had a family cemetery built on the land so all Chester had to do was dig two shallow graves and no one would ever know. I'd come up with a good story to tell too. Chester would take the fall for my missing child. Her DNA would be all over him and I would play the role of the distraught mother. It was simple no one would ever suspect me.

He was the one who had been stalking me and Ava. I'd run to the police and tell them that he'd attacked me and taken my child as soon as I was done with Delores. I never thought she would turn on me. She had always had my back but goes to show you can't really trust anyone. I'd brought her into my home after all those years even after she stuck her nose in something she had nothing to do with and she crossed me.

Delores was still knocked out cold. She had a few scrapes and bruises. The sweat suit I had put on her was ripped and torn from the beating I had given her once I caught her ass. I looked at her with disdain. I wanted to kill her right then and there but I wanted her to suffer like I had suffered when she had kidnapped my daughter and stolen my damn car.

I slapped her with all my might across her face causing her eyes to shoot open and look around into the moist dimly lit basement.

"Yes," I said drawing her attention to me as I towered over her weak frail body. "Wake up you old ungrateful bitch." I spat as I leaned in closer so she could look into my eyes.

I sensed no fear in her. That pissed me off. I was the one who had the upper hand. She should have been sitting there begging me to allow her to live. Who the hell did she think she was to not show me the respect I deserved? I was the one standing over her. She was tied up with nowhere to go. She didn't have it in her to do the things that I could do.

I picked up a rusty screwdriver that lay on the floor and drove it into her thigh. She let out an agonizing howl as her body jerked in pain.

"That's right bitch show some damn respect," I shouted in her face.

Delores hauled off and spit in my face as tears streamed down her face. I immediately hauled off and smacked the hell out of her with the screwdriver in my hand trying to knock her teeth down her throat.

"You want to spit in my face?" I challenged as I laid another vicious blow to her dome opening up a cut over her left eye. She winced but did not make a sound. "So you're a tough old bitch?" I asked annoyed by her refusal to bow down to me.

She had worked for my family for many years. She was to treat me with respect. I was better than her.

"Ms. Marteen," she said in between a cynical laugh. Blood covered her teeth and ran down the side of her mouth. "The evil Ms. Marteen." She said still laughing and taunting me.

I went into a blind rage destroying everything around me in the basement. She was mocking me. I was not to be mocked. Her life was at stake and she dared to mock me? She obviously had a death wish. She would get that wish granted soon enough but on my time. As much as I wanted to bash her skull in I didn't hit her.

She stared at me as I slung things around, slamming them to the ground cursing her. She didn't flinch the compassion I once saw for me in her eyes was gone. She had stopped loving me. That was okay because the feeling was mutual I had stopped loving that old bitch too. If it weren't for me she would have been dead long ago.

"You ungrateful old bitch," I said as spit flew out of my mouth and landed onto her lip. "You will respect me!" WHAM! I popped her upside her head causing it to jerk back and the chair to rock. "Do you think you can take me?" I challenged.

She was old, worn, and beaten. The weakest link she didn't have what it took to handle me. I kicked her in the chest knocking her backwards in the chair sending her hitting the pavement with a sickening thud. She groaned as her eyelids fluttered and she slipped into unconsciousness.

Kneeling to the ground beside her and leaning towards her ear I whispered. "Maybe when you wake up you will show me the respect I deserve." Then she was out.

I began to pace back and forth. Chester had been gone for far too long. I pulled out my cell phone and walked up the dark basement stairs and into the kitchen dialing Chester's telephone number. He picked up on the first ring.

"Where the hell are you?" I demanded before he could say hello.

"Marteen I cannot find her. I have looked in every vacant house over here and I don't see her. I got a call from the precinct I need to go in for a minute," he explained.

"Listen goddamnit!" I said becoming angry. "I don't give a damn who you got a call from you need to find my fucking daughter!" I yelled into the phone.

There was silence on the other end of the phone. If that idiot went to that precinct before handling his business he would be in for a bigger surprise than being set up I'd be burying him in that cemetery with the other two.

"Hello?" I hollered as I looked at my phone to make sure he hadn't ended our conversation.

Sighing he said, "I'm here Marteen."

"Go find her now!" I said before I ended the call myself. I couldn't depend on anyone for shit except myself. Who couldn't find a little blonde hair gray eyed three year old? It couldn't have been too hard to do.

My phone started to ring it was Chester. "You found her!" I said feeling a bit of relief answering the phone.

Stuttering he said no. He was just calling to tell me he would look for her as soon as he came back from speaking with the Sergeant. He tried to explain his job was on the line. What did his job being on the line have to do with me? He had ample opportunities to back out of our plan he didn't give a damn about his job when he was running around trying to kidnap Ava or when he walked up those stairs to kill my daughter.

Now all of a sudden he had to do the right thing and report to work as instructed. I didn't want to hear any of his explaining I told him I would find Yasmine my damn self but he'd better be at the house when I got back or he'd be worrying about more than his job before hanging up the phone.

I shook my head annoyed by his dumb ass. I got into my dad's Mercedes and headed to my destination. I took the long way so I could drive by my home only to see a swarm of police had the entire street blocked off.

"Fuck!" I shouted banging my hand on the steering wheel. The wheels in my head began to turn as I envisioned the story I would have to tell regarding what had went down in my home. Perry had seen Chester there he would be my witness. He had experienced Chester's standoffish demeanor he could vouch for me that Chester wasn't a man to be trusted.

He'd even asked me if I would be okay alone with Chester still there. I could tell the police I was afraid, that he had attacked Ms. Delores and forced me to go along with the plan. I could say I tried to give Perry hints to call the police before he left but Chester had been sitting right there I didn't want all of us to be harmed.

I searched those houses for hours on end there was no sign of Yasmine. I called Chester several times but never got an answer. I headed back to my parents home. So many thoughts were clouding my head I couldn't function. I wondered why he wasn't answering his damn phone. I was becoming more irate by the second. When I did see him I would tear his illiterate behind a brand new asshole.

When I reached the basement Delores was still laying in the overturned chair. I could see she was still breathing maybe just taking a much needed rest. She was about to get her ass up. My nerves were bad I was trembling in anger. Playtime was over no need in toying with her anymore it was time for her to meet her maker.

I kicked her fragile body. "Wake your ass up," I said kicking her again with a little more force behind it. She opened her eyes and stared at me.

She whispered something I couldn't quite make out. I knelt down beside her to hear her better when I felt a sharp pain in my shoulder. I screamed in pain. She had managed to loosen the rope we had tied her with and had the rusty screwdriver I used to stab her twisting it in my arm.

I punched her with my other hand snapping her neck back as blood gushed from her nose some splattering on my face. She let go of the screw driver. I pulled it out slowly. Surprisingly I felt no pain. The initial entrance of the foreign object surprised me more than it hurt. She was loose but she still was no match for me I was stronger and faster than she was.

Delores scrambled to her feet and took off running towards the stairs. I was impressed she moved fairly fast for a woman her age. I trotted after her allowing her to get a head start. I enjoyed the game of cat and mouse she played. She would eventually be devoured. She lost her footing halfway up the stairs and slid down a couple before she scrambled back to her feet and took off again.

"How far do you think you're going to get Delores?" I called after her.

She didn't respond or look back she continued her attempt to escape. It was inevitable she wouldn't get far. "Where are you going to go?" I taunted laughing to myself. I knew our property inside and out every inch of it. I had lived there my entire life and had still spent quite a lot of time there as an adult.

She was good at hiding but I was much better at seeking. I thought I heard something in the kitchen. I opened the drawer to the console table and pulled out my father's .38. Tiptoeing I burst through the door in the kitchen only to find it empty. "Come on out Delores," I said in the sweetest voice I could muster. "I promise I won't hurt you," I lied.

I held my breath hoping to hear something from somewhere. I turned on the lights as I entered each room searching for her. I knew she couldn't have gotten out because I had locked all the doors from the inside just in case something went wrong. She'd have to break a window if she wanted to get out of the estate and I hadn't heard any glass shattering.

"I'm sorry for hurting you," I yelled. I noticed her shoes barely showing from behind the sofa in the family room. I walked softly before jumping behind the sofa and letting off a single shot that entered the hardwood floor. She wasn't there only the shoes she once had covering her feet. She was playing the survival game very well.

"Cute," I said to myself. How witty of her to buy herself some time and find out my exact location. She was trying to toy with me but it was a losing battle she didn't have the brain power to outsmart me. If anything she gave herself away there was only one route from the family she could have gone without running into me and only three rooms she could hide in.

I smiled as I stalked her in the mansion she'd raised me in. "I'm going to fiinnnddd yoouuuu," I sang as I made my way through the double doors that lead to her hiding place.

I listened intently as I entered each room. I could hear breathing coming from the closet in the guest bedroom. I turned on the light and taunted her some more. She had to have known that I would find her. I opened the closet door and BAM was hit with the heel of a shoe in the middle of my forehead. I could feel a couple of trickles of blood flow from the open wound followed by a more steady flow of warm blood falling down my face.

She was putting up a good fight. As she tried to run past me I caught her by the matted bunch of naps that sat on top of her head snatching her backwards and down to the floor. I started to pound on her and was taken aback when she began to pound back blocking a mirage of my shots. She wasn't making things easy for me.

In the midst of the altercation I had dropped the gun sending it to sliding across the floor. She'd hit me with a good shot to the nose making me stall for a brief second. Delores scrambled towards the gun but I jumped on her back. Her body went flat as her face slammed into the floor with a crunch. I rolled her over her nose was twisted in an awkward manner. I had broken her nose.

I banged her head against the hardwood floor as she continued to spread her fingers out for the gun. I leaned forward snatching it up and pointing at her at point blank range. I pulled the trigger as she pushed up with all her might knocking me off balance as the gun fired into the ceiling bringing down a little debris and somehow ricocheting through the bedroom window with a loud shatter.

We struggled for control of the pistol Delores slamming my hand hard against the floor knocking the gun out of my hand again and by chance only knocking me on my back. She snatched up the gun both of us now standing on two feet facing one another. Somebody had to make a move. Delores wasn't about to shoot me. If she did she wouldn't kill me. The way her hands trembled as she held the gun on me let me know she still feared for her life which gave me the upper hand.

"Make a move," I said out of breath. That's when Delores closed her eyes and pulled the trigger. Wrong move old bitch I thought as I charged her as the hot lead ripped through my side. I felt it burning but it didn't stop me I continued forward as she let off another shot sending me to the ground.

I wasn't fading I was just fine. The pain wasn't unbearable she wouldn't get away from me. She stood above me looking down like she had power over me. I laughed in her face. I laughed so hard my stomach hurt as she stared into my eyes.

"You will never be able to hurt anyone ever again," she spoke as tears ran down her face. I wanted to get up but I couldn't. My body wouldn't allow me to move.

She turned to leave the room. I lay there trying to muster enough strength to get up and go after her but I couldn't. I was too weak. Marteen LeBlanc weak? I pounded my fist against the floor splashing around the puddle of blood that I lay in. A few minutes later Delores was back with a gas can pouring the strong liquid all around the room.

I managed to roll myself over and slide on my stomach like a snake to her leg. I pulled at her leg. She looked down and kicked me back over.

"No more!" she yelled with more strength than I ever heard her speak with. "This ends now you rotten little bitch!" she said spitting on me for the second time that night. With that she struck a match tossing it in the corner of the room, limping out and never looking back.

## LAUREN

## (22)

I didn't know what the hell was going on with Chaz but whatever it was I didn't want any parts of it. I instructed the cab driver to take me to a hotel downtown and wait outside for my return. I allowed the bellhop to help me bring my things up to the room and went back downstairs. I was tired but my mind wouldn't let me rest. If I stayed in that room I would be on edge all night. If I tried to go to sleep I would be tossing and turning. It was a no win situation for me.

As the driver dropped me off at my car I decided to go back to the hospital to visit my daddy. Sure he had told me to go home and I most definitely didn't want to run into my mother again but I needed to see him. He had heard only half of my story I wanted to tell him just between him and I why I was doing what I was doing. When my mother pulled all my skeletons out of the closet I could see the hurt on my father's face.

I never wanted to disappoint him my father was a wonderful man. He loved me; he respected and had always wanted nothing but the best for me. He'd stayed with my mother all those years for me. Not because he loved her. He knew that she wasn't shit. She was a no good ass bitch. I hated her. I'd never say those words aloud but all the things she'd subjected me to I should have hated her. I really should have beaten that bitch down.

She was jealous of me always had been. I believed she had secretly wanted to be me but she could never be the woman I had become. She wasn't a go getter she didn't have the drive or the looks to accomplish the things I had over the years. She could kiss my ass though she didn't have anything coming from me. As soon as my daddy was cleared to go home she wouldn't have anything coming from him either.

I sat in my parked car smoking a cigarette outside the hospital. I'd started smoking only a few months ago to calm my nerves. I even partook in smoking weed just to take the edge off when I had a date. I sat there thinking. As much shit as I talked about getting money I didn't like sleeping with men to get.

I thought about Dollar and how much money he made off his bitches. I could start my own escort service show my girls the ins and outs of the business mold them into every mans fantasies while building my own empire. I would treat my women well because I was a woman I was in their shoes once upon a time. If they chose to live such a life what better woman to show them how to get money than me?

I'd even provide incentives like a real job. You max out for the month bring in so much money you get a bonus for your efforts. The working girl that made the most money at the end of the quarter got an all expense paid vacation to the destination of their choice for a week. I was thinking big. I always thought big. That is what separated me from the average hoe. While I had chosen, while I was being pimped I didn't soak up the game I soaked up his game and planned on taking it to the next level.

I hated being in hospitals they stank. They smelled of sick people and death to me. I didn't like to see people deteriorating. It tugged at my heart actually made me afraid. I couldn't imagine the pain they went through. I couldn't imagine what daddy had been going through. They poked and prodded him all times of night. To be honest he didn't get sick until he started treatment.

I rounded the corner to stop at the vending machines that were near the cafeteria. I was looking down at my cell phone when I ran into someone. My eyes were still on the ground. I took in the alligator shoes, the slacks, and the button down shirt all the way up to the handsome brown face my eyes began to widen. I started to back up thinking this nigga had been following me the entire time.

He wasn't about to get me in the hospital. I wasn't a snitch or anything but he would damn sure end up going to jail in that mothafucka because I was going to cause a scene. He stared down at me his 6'4" frame still intimidating. The way he was looking at me wasn't threatening at all but if I knew Dollar I knew that he could change in a split second.

"Chill out," he said reaching out to me. I continued to back up until my back hit the wall. I didn't blink for fear that I might've had to fight for my life. Now was not the time I was drained.

"Now is not the time Dollar," I said keeping my eyes planted directly on his. A doctor walked past and I thought about asking him for help. My heart pounded. Looking at him I missed him and hated him all at the same time.

He had showed me more money than I ever had thought imaginable but he had exploited me in the process. Dollar didn't give a damn about anyone but himself. I was his bottom bitch but he didn't love me anymore than he loved them bitches he kept doped up on pills and who knows what else.

He loved what I could do for him. I was being wise I knew not to get that twisted.

"I know Choc," he said. I hadn't known him that long but we had spent a lot of time together and he seemed to be troubled. "Listen, I really have to talk to you."

I didn't have time to talk to him about business or anything else. I was still pissed he had decided to put his hands on me and try to keep me from my father who was fucking dying. He could save all the bullshit. Although he put on a good game face Dollar was full of shit he saw an opportunity to gain and he jumped on it. I wasn't anyone's fool. I had been the fool for far too long.

I had to hand it to him though he'd helped me find my strength. "I have to go check on my father," I said turning to walk away.

"It's about Ava," he called after me causing me to spin around with fire in my eyes. What the hell did him and his brother do to my damn friend? It was one thing to mess with me. I had put myself in that position but Ava had been through enough.

"What about Ava," I snapped walking up on him. He threw his hands up. I looked up at his big ass unafraid and ready to go as hard as my body would allow me to. "If you and your punk ass bro-"he cut me off just as two men passed us by heading for the exit.

"She's in a room in the emergency department," he said walking towards the exit as well. "I don't have time to talk right now call me later." He said rushing out the door.

What in the hell was going on? I stared after him not knowing if I should follow him or head to the emergency room to check on my best friend. I opted to deal with him later. I needed to make sure my girl was good and to check on my daddy.

I made it to the ER department just as Dollar's brother and a beautiful little girl were coming through the double doors. I stared him down as I approached him not giving a damn about the little girl he held in his arms.

"What the hell did you and your brother do to Ava?" I questioned poking him in the chest. The little girl looked afraid as she buried her head in his chest. I felt sorry for her and immediately regretted approaching him in such a manner. I did have a heart somewhere in my body. I used to be that frightened little girl once upon a time.

Before he could answer a beautiful older woman came out behind him. "Dr. Powers you take care now. We will make sure that Ava is okay." She whispered and then turned to me as if to ask who I was all up in their business.

I didn't care how old she was or that she worked at the hospital she'd better straighten her ass the hell up. "Pam," he said clearly exhausted. "This is Lauren," he paused. "Ava's best friend can you take her back there for a minute I called her here to sit with her for a while." He lied.

Maybe he wasn't so bad after all but then again who knew what he was capable of. All the shit that had been going on in all of our lives lately who could a woman trust these days. Pam or whatever her name was looked back at me and smiled. *Fake ass bitch* I thought as I plastered on a fake smile of my own.

"Follow me sweetheart I will take you right to her," she said leading the way through the secured double doors. I took the short stroll to a small room to find Ava hooked up to a few machines and sleeping soundly. Pam smiled and exited the room.

I whispered Ava's name causing her to stir and moan. I waited for a response but she fell back asleep. I watched her as she rested peacefully. I sat there for a while wondering what had landed my friend in the hospital. She looked like she had been drug the mud that night. They needed to get her up to a room and bathed so she could rest more comfortably.

As the fatigue began to settle in my body I must have dozed off because I was startled when I'd heard the door open and saw a police officer walking in. Ava woke up as well her eyes opened wide as the officer tried to tell me I needed to get out of the room he had some questions he needed for her to answer.

I could sense something was wrong by her response. She challenged him directly never looking away as her nostrils flared and she forced herself to sit up in the bed despite the pain medication that she'd been given earlier.

"And what kind of questions might you need to ask me officer?" she said with sarcasm. "Maybe about how you attacked me and tried to kill me?" she said never taking her eyes off of him.

He looked confused as he told her she must not be feeling too well he was there to take a statement. "Oh no you are him," she said in between gritted teeth. Before he could respond nurse Pam came in and asked him what he was doing in her room. He tried to give her the same bullshit ass answer which put her on alert.

"I'm sorry officer," she said reading the name on his badge. "Bloomfield she has already spoken with two detectives she needs her rest and you will not disturb her." She stood there and opened the door wide for him to make his exit. "Now you need to leave or I will have to call someone to have you escorted out." She stated with a lot more attitude than I could not have imagined she was capable of giving.

He hesitated before he began to make steps towards the door. He was jittery very nervous which made me uneasy. Before he left he turned to Ava to tell her that they would be talking very soon.

"Not if I can help it you bastard," Ava spat.

That was all nurse Pam needed to hear before she was on her walkie talkie calling for backup. She wasn't playing. I sat there looking confused Officer Bloomfield if he really was an officer high tailed it up out of there with Nurse Pam on his heels giving her backup a detailed description and his every move.

Ava sat there fuming. I didn't know what any of that shit was about but I had an eerie feeling that he would be back. I wanted to see my dad but I didn't want to leave Ava in that room alone. I gave my friend a minute to get herself together.

"Lauren you've got to get me out of here. I don't know how the hell he found me but if I stay in this hospital room I am a sitting duck I might not make it through the night." She said in a panic as she motioned for me to get her clothing.

Despite the doctor's orders I was going to help her slip out. I couldn't have her in that hospital and people were stalking her. As I helped her get on her clothes I urged her to let me know what was going on. I needed to know what I was getting myself into. Either way I was still riding with my best friend I just needed to know how nasty the situation could get.

The hospital was pretty dead they were short staffed and it was like a ghost town. When we slipped out of the room it was easy for us to make our way down the corridor and out to the parking lot. When we got in the car Ava let out a loud sigh. I had never seen her on edge and I didn't like it at all.

That bitch Marteen had a couple things coming to her. What Ava didn't know is I had been doing a lot of dirt and getting away with it. Kat and the twins were the first I had handled but there had been a few more afterwards. As I thought about it hell I had turned into Dollar in a female form. I didn't know if that was a good or bad thing but it was my thang.

I was going to handle the situation for her. I guess I did need to call Dollar. There was never a situation I didn't handle without him. Now it was time for me to pimp him for his services. Funny how life was, things could change in an instance. Those mothafuckas wanted to stalk somebody that could definitely be done. I was good at stalking prey. I just needed to get Ava someplace safe and handle that punk ass cop and that yellow bitch Marteen.

I knew exactly who she was. I had enjoyed the few dates I had with her father. He was a weird ass bastard liked to get cucumbers and dildos stuck up his ass. He would say I'm not a faggot. Not that I had anything against gay men but he most definitely was what he proclaimed not to be. I don't give a damn how sexual or how much of a freak you are. No straight man should ever want anything shoved up his ass.

He'd pay me a nice amount of money to do so. Every client I had ever slept with I secretly recorded our little rendezvous just in case I had to use it as leverage against them in the future. They were high profile people who could make or break the average hoe. Not this one. I was two steps ahead of the game.

I shook my head thinking how small the world really was. Our town wasn't small it wasn't all that big either but it was large enough for none of us to have to ever cross paths. Everything happened for a reason. The reason for these paths to have crossed was to take the LeBlanc family down and anyone who stood in our way.

I called Dollar asking him where he was at. He said he had handled what he'd needed to handle and was on his way to his spot. When I told him Ava was with me he damn near lost his mind. Started carrying on about how hardheaded she was and asking me why I let her leave.

I had to check him let him know shit had gotten a lot more serious since he had left. I glanced over at Ava who had fallen asleep in the passenger seat. I whispered about the events that had just taken place. He cursed under his breath saying he needed to call Cameron.

Not really wanting his brother in my mix like that I told him to just hold out until we met up. I had a couple things I needed to run past him first. He hesitated for a moment it took a little finessing before he agreed on my terms. It was time to make some major moves.

# AVA

## (23)

I loved my girl Lauren to death but if she thought I was going to sit around and wait for someone to come after me she had another thing coming. Marteen and Mr. Bloomfield had been stalking both me and my children. They had me bent backwards. It would be a cold day in hell when I allowed someone to harass me and children and not suffer the consequences.

If Marteen wanted to play the game of life I would play with her but not in the way she was anticipating. I needed to rest all of the stress from the past few months was taking a toll on my body and I could potentially miscarry my baby but I had to put an end to everything that was happening to me before I could be at peace.

I loved the child that was growing inside of me and I wanted to be with Cameron but I'd be damned if I waited for them to attack me again. I had given Marteen too many passes. I had tried to be a woman about the situation and think logically but the time had come for "A" to show her face. Anyone could make it out of the trenches but for some of us that lifestyle never left we could resort back to being the product of our environment at anytime.

I listened to Lauren whispering to Kymani aka Dollar on the telephone. Lauren always came up with the biggest schemes. I'd let her lay some of her cards on the table before I let her know I had been playing possum the entire time and wanted in. We pulled up to a posh hotel downtown when Lauren nudged me to get up.

"I'm up," I said my eyes still closed head resting against the window.

Looking at me and shaking her head she knew what was up. "How long have you been up?" she asked.

"Long enough to let you know I want in." I said opening my eyes and looking at her seriously. She laughed a little as she tried to reason with me saying I was in no position to be going through anymore bullshit as she placed her hand on my stomach. I was pregnant but that was all the more reason for me to be involved.

Although I wanted to have the baby growing inside of me I had three other children to live for. If no one could understand that then fuck them because I had a score to settle in the worst way. Marteen might have been a crazy bitch but she wasn't 'bout the life I was planning on bringing to her. She might have been able to pull that shit with them L 7 ass bitches she was used to being around but not with me. I was built from a different breed.

I didn't give a damn who her family was. They bled just like everyone else. I refused to allow her to keep fucking with me based off her father's reputation. If he wanted some he could get it too. Mafia affiliation or not I had a right to protect me and mines and this bitch had taken her jealous and obsessive ways to a whole other level.

She could play crazy all day every day. That was fine with me but the bitch had better get ready to for the ride I was about to take her on.

"Lauren, I know you mean well," I started. "But if you don't take me with you I guarantee I am not staying here and I will handle these mothafuckas with or without you." I stated firmly.

She sighed putting the car in drive and heading to Dollar's. I called Cameron. He had a fit when he found out I had left the hospital. He asked how I got past Pam and I had to go through all the details about Officer Bloomfield bringing his ass up there and lightweight threatening me.

Livid would have been an understatement for how Cam was feeling when I told him how things had went down. I was thankful Lauren was in that room. Wasn't no telling where I would be had he caught me sleeping without any witnesses around in my state. I stayed on the phone while he called up to the hospital asking for Pam. I heard him going through a series of questions before he came back on the mobile line with me.

"What's wrong?" I asked concerned. From what I'd heard no one had seen Ms. Pam. It wasn't like her to stay away from her post for long. I didn't have a good feeling about that. I silently prayed nothing bad had happened to her because of me. I was getting everybody around me into all kinds of shit.

"Don't worry about that right now," Cameron said changing the subject. I could tell he was worried as well. I told him we were meeting at Dollars house in about fifteen minutes. He asked who was we. I told him Lauren and me. He laughed.

If I didn't have so much on my mind I would have laughed too. How in the hell did her and Dollar go through all that shit earlier and now they were working together like the modern day Bonnie and Clyde ready to do some dirt. Those two nutcases deserved each other. Too each his or her own I thought as I shook my head and leaned back to enjoy the rest of the ride.

When we pulled up to the house Cameron's car was already parked outside. I took a deep breath as we walked up to the door. Before we could knock the door flew open and we were instructed to hurry inside by the Spanish chick I had seen earlier when I helped Lauren escape. As we entered her and Lauren exchanged nasty looks at one another.

I didn't feel like anymore drama so I pushed Lauren forward towards the living room where I heard the voices of Dollar and Cameron. We didn't need any more unnecessary drama. Whatever they had against each other would have to take a backseat.

When I entered the room Cameron stood to greet me with a hug. He pretended to scold me for being hardheaded. I shrugged my shoulders tilting my head to the side giving him my "oh hell oh well" look. He laughed and urged me to take a seat. I didn't want to sit down though. I was antsy. I was ready to get things rolling. I was done playing games. I didn't have a game plan the first so it was best I sat my ass down and listened to what they had and we'd figure out what we needed to do to shut shit down so our lives could go back to normal.

Lauren started off the conversation with some shit that blew my mind. I mean I knew there could only be one reason why she had been fooling around with Dollar but to hear her talk about prostituting had me tripping. What was really crazy was the fact she'd had several "dates" with Marteen's father. Who in essence was an undercover brother.

She pulled out a little device and pressed play. On the screen was Lauren and Mr. LeBlanc engaging in some serious homosexual activity. I mean she was tearing his ass up had him bent over with a strap-on banging that mans back out. We all sat there cringing as Lauren sat back with her arms spread out wrapped around the back of the couch legs propped up smiling at her performance.

Dollar looked at her like she was crazy. "Choc, you know better," he said angry that she was videotaping his clients.

Lauren gave him the screw face shooing him off with her hand. "I gotta cover my own ass," she said rolling her neck and smacking her lips. Cameron and I sat there looking at the pair go back and forth about this hooking business as if we weren't even sitting there.

I marveled for a moment at Lauren. If I hadn't known that he was pimpin' my girl I would have given him props. She was always a good shit talker but never was she down for the cause when shit got dangerous. Lauren had been the type to stand in the background and talk shit while everyone else did the dirty work.

I never got upset with her about that in the past because I knew that to be her our entire lives. She didn't fake the funk either she would let you know ahead of time when it was time to get down to business she wasn't going to do shit. I couldn't do anything but respect that. I knew exactly where she stood I didn't have to question anything with Lauren.

But this new bitch that was sitting before me she was a piece of work. I was impressed. She was standing her ground I couldn't believe my eyes. I sat there watching them go back and forth with a smirk on my face. Dollar was trying to explain how her videotaping his clients were bad for business if anyone ever found out she was doing that his entire empire would fold.

Her argument consisted of her letting him know that she always had to look out for self. Contrary to what he might have believed in his head his business wasn't really his business it was hers and every other working girl he had turning tricks business was hers too. So he could either deal with it or find another line of work because if any one of "his" clients crossed her they would be all over the news stations.

I could tell Dollar was becoming angry so I decided to step in before they started acting a fool like they were earlier.

"Okay lovebirds can we get back down to business?" I said.

"Amen!" Cameron yelled rolling his eyes. I could tell he wasn't interested in what the pair had going on. Truth be told I wasn't either.

We sat around that table for hours. Dollar had done his research. The detectives that had showed up at the hospital were on Chester's ass never could get anything to stick on him. The streets were talking and most of the time the streets were right about what they had to say.

Chester and Marteen had been old flings many years ago. Recently they'd hooked up and started some twisted little love affair with Marteen manipulating him into doing her dirty work. This was stalking me and anything else she requested of him to help her get Cameron back.

What Marteen didn't know was that Officer Bloomfield was into some other shit as well. He was pushing more dope through the city than a body pumped blood. He had a small army of other dirty cops who helped him along with a couple hood niggas. They would rob other drug dealers or scare them out of their cash by threatening to crack down on their operation if they didn't agree to a 70/30 split Chester getting the 70.

Shit was getting ugly for Chester. "One nigga particularly named Chaz had started an uprising. It was quoted he had said "I ain't laying down for nan nigga." Dollar said causing Lauren and I look at each other. This shit was a whole lot deeper than what the fuck I'd expected. I had been living the square life I didn't need those types of problems. Lauren squirmed in her seat. She had a thing for Chaz and now she was worried.

It was one thing for them to funk with other niggas in the streets but dirty ass cops that was an entirely different story. I didn't know where Dollar was getting his information but it sounded just like the Johnson brothers to take Chester's antics personally and refuse to fold under pressure. We spent the majority of the night talking about how to rid my life of Chester and that crazy bitch Marteen.

I wouldn't say it a loud but I was ready to seriously hurt someone. The Hispanic broad Maria stood in the doorway the entire time trying to ear hustle. I made it a point to ask Cameron about her I didn't like the look in her eyes. Something was up with her she wasn't loyal she was a snake.

I was usually a pretty good judge of character and that one had to go. I nudged Lauren nodding towards Maria. "Wassup with your girl over there?" I said as we burned holes through each other with our eyes.

Lauren shrugged her off saying the bitch was retarded and don't pay her any mind. However, I wasn't feeling how she was staring at me. I was tempted to ask her what the problem was until breaking news popped up on the television. I could tell Lauren knew something because she sat there quietly trembling on the sofa next to me.

"Choc?" Dollar said staring at her with concern. She was in a daze. "Chocolate!" he yelled a little louder snapping her out of her trance.

"Huh?" she said still staring at the T.V.

"Wassup?" he asked eyeing her closely. "You aight?"

She stumbled over her words as she told him that she was okay. I jumped in the conversation to take the heat off of her explaining we grew up in the projects the shooting happened in. Those two off duty police officers were dead and Lauren knew something about it.

I excused Lauren and myself to go outside saying I needed some fresh air. As soon as we got outside I closed the door behind us and peeked through the window to make sure no one was listening.

"You know them?" I asked after making sure no one was within earshot.

That is when she broke it down to me about Marcus, Chaz and the shootout that had broken out earlier. All I could say was damn. I didn't know who's predicament was worse mine or my "brothers". I needed to holler at Chaz and Marcus. They knew firsthand about the kind of monster I was dealing with. They had a lot of muscle they could be useful to my cause.

We tried to call Chaz's phone but it kept going to voicemail. My stomach started to feel queasy.

"I need to tell Cameron," I said heading back inside the house. Lauren grabbed my arm like she was crazy.

"You don't need to tell Cameron shit," she snapped. "You are going to put an outsider in Chaz's business like that?" she said as I watched anger build up inside of her.

Looking down at her hand gripping on to my arm I took a deep breath and counted to ten before I responded. I was taking into consideration everyone was on edge, tired and we had all had a rough day. I loved the fact that Lauren had found her voice but she needn't get it twisted I was true to this not new to this and I would straighten her right on out and or including laying her out if need be pregnant and all.

"The outsider you are talking about is the father of my child," I stated calmly looking down at my stomach and back up at her.

She had the nerve to smack her lips and roll her eyes and bring up the fact that Rodney was my baby daddy too and he wasn't shit either. I always knew Lauren had problems but she was going a little far talking to me sideways. We had fallen out a time or two before because of her slick mouth. I got it I knew she had feelings for Chaz and wanted to protect him from who I didn't know but if that was the issue that was all she had to say.

It was simple she didn't have to go where she was going with it.

"I'm going to pretend as if we never had this conversation Lauren so we can remain friends," I said snatching my arm away from her and busting through the door. It would be a long time before I spoke to that bitch she was getting besides herself. She must have forgotten that I wasn't the bitch to fuck with. I could hang with the best of them.

I stepped into the living room plopping down on the couch fuming. "Well damn what in the world is wrong with you?" Dollar asked.

I didn't say a word just shook my head. If I opened my mouth what came out wasn't going to be nothing nice so as opposed to adding fuel to the fire I held my tongue.

Everyone sat in the room in silence looking dumb. When I became angry I became impatient. We sat in there all fucking morning and hadn't come up with one damn game plan. My brain began to warm up as hundreds of thoughts filled my head. I sat on the edge on the couch and began speaking. It was time to set our game plan in motion.

I spoke slowly and deliberately so Cam and Dollar both understood me carefully. Just like that I had mastered a plan to take Chester down for good. At first neither one of them were with it but when I explained to them especially Dollar the amount of money he would make from the deal it was too sweet for him to pass up.

I glanced back at Maria standing in the doorway and called her over. I didn't like the bitch but I could definitely use her help with this shit. I could see in her eyes that she was a shady bitch that couldn't be trusted. For the time being she would be on team Ava until she didn't need to be on "A" team anymore which would be all good because I didn't need the bitch for long anyway. To me she was expendable.

Cameron stared at me in amazement. He had seen yet another side of me and I could tell he was digging it a little bit. Cam and Dollar dapped each other up as I wrapped up the plan looking everyone in the eye so they would know their position and how to play it. Lauren stood staring at me hotter than a six shooter.

I really wasn't tripping over what Lauren was feeling or what she had to say. My concern was the safety of me and mine. I would never put Chaz and Marcus out there like that by telling anyone in detail about the things they did. People always folded when they were facing 25 to life. The hardest niggas on the planet acted like little bitches. I'd seen it many times.

Dollar and Cameron knew just enough about them to play out their portion of my plan the rest was up to Maria and I. Lauren or Chocolate as they called her wasn't a part of the plan. She could continue to live in her reality television world and play the victim of her own circumstances. Enough was enough I was over it. If it meant we fell out then so be it. I had been there for her unconditionally on numerous occasions she had yet to do the same for me.

*…..To be continued…..*

# ABOUT THE AUTHOR

Keima Campbell has been writing since the sixth grade. She was recently encouraged by fans of her short stories to try her hand at writing a novel. Coming up with an exciting and gritty novel called That Woman's Husband. She was born in Topeka, Kansas and has had the opportunity to live in Missouri, California, Texas, D.C., and Florida. She now resides in the Metro Atlanta, Georgia area with her four children and is working on the sequel to That Woman's Husband called Strip Clubs and Dollar Bill and Mean Green the final installment of the Chosen Trilogy, as well a short story series called Bathroom Pics about an internet dating site. You can reach this author at Skyenovels@gmail.com and also order your e-book at www.amazon.com as well as paperback copies at both www.amazon.com and www.createspace.com/4134796.